THE DROP
and
THE LIST

Also by Mick Herron

Jackson Lamb thrillers

Slow Horses
Dead Lions
Real Tigers
Spook Street
London Rules
Joe Country

Zoë Boehm thrillers

Down Cemetery Road
The Last Voice You Hear
Why We Die
Smoke and Whispers

Reconstruction
Nobody Walks
This Is What Happened

THE DROP
and
THE LIST

Two Slough House Novellas

MICK
HERRON

JOHN MURRAY

The List first published in Great Britain in 2015 by Soho Press

First published by John Murray (Publishers) in 2017
An Hachette UK company

The Drop first published in Great Britain in 2018 by John Murray
(Publishers)

This paperback edition published in 2019

6

A CIP catalogue record for this title is
available from the British Library

Paperback ISBN 9781529327311

Typeset in Bembo by Palimpsest Book Production Limited,
Falkirk, Stirlingshire

Printed and bound in Great Britain by Clays Ltd, Elcograf S.p.A.

John Murray policy is to use papers that are natural, renewable
and recyclable products and made from wood grown in sustainable
forests. The logging and manufacturing processes are expected to
conform to the environmental regulations of the country of origin.

John Murray (Publishers)
Carmelite House
50 Victoria Embankment
London EC4Y 0DZ

www.johnmurray.co.uk

THE LIST

THOSE WHO KNEW him said it was how he'd have wanted to go. Dieter Hess died in his armchair, surrounded by his books; a half-full glass of 2008 Burgundy at his elbow, a half-smoked Montecristo in the ashtray on the floor. In his lap, Yeats's *Collected* – the yellow-jacketed Macmillan edition – and in the CD tray Pärt's *Für Alina*, long hushed by the time Bachelor found the body, but its lingering silences implicit in the air, settling like dust on faded surfaces. Those who knew him said it was how he'd have wanted to go, but John Bachelor suspected Dieter would sooner have drunk more wine, read a little longer, and finished his cigar. Dieter had been sick, but he hadn't been tired of life. Out of respect, or possibly mild superstition, Bachelor waited a while in that quiet room, thinking about their relationship – professional but friendly – before nodding to himself, as if satisfied Dieter had cleared the finishing line, and calling Regent's Park. Dieter was long retired from the world of spooks, but there were protocols to be observed. When a spy passes, his cupboards need clearing out.

There was a wake, though nobody called it that. Most of the attendees had never known Dieter Hess, or the world he'd moved in as an Active; they rode desks at Regent's Park, and his death was simply an excuse for a drink and a little stress relief. If they had to come over pious at the name of a dead German who'd fed them titbits in the Old Days – which were either Good or Bad, depending on the speaker – that was fine. So as the evening wore on the gathering split into two, the larger group issuing regular gales of laughter and ordering ever more idiosyncratic rounds of drinks, and the smaller huddling in a nook off the main bar and talking about Dieter, and other Actives now defunct, and quietly pickling itself in its past.

The pub was off Great Portland Street; nicely traditional-looking from the road, and not too buggered about inside. John Bachelor had never been here before – for reasons that probably don't need spelling out, Regent's Park had never settled on a local – but had developed affection for it over the previous two and a quarter hours. Dieter too had faded into a warm memory. In life, like many of Bachelor's charges, the old man could be prickly and demanding, but now that his complaints of not enough money and too little regard had been silenced by a heart no longer merely dicky but well and truly dicked, Bachelor had no trouble dwelling on his good points. This was a man, after all, who had risked his life for his ideals. German by birth, then East German by dint of geopolitics, Dieter Hess had supplied the Park with classified information during two dark decades, and if his product – largely to do with troop movements: Hess had worked in the Transport Ministry – had never swayed policy or scooped up hidden treasure, the man responsible deserved respect . . . Bachelor had reached that maudlin state where he was measuring his worth against those who'd gone before him, and his own career had been neither stellar nor dangerous. That his current berth was known as the milk round summed it up. John Bachelor's charges were retired assets, which is to say those who'd come in from other nations' colds; who'd served their time in that peculiar shadowland where clerical work and danger meet. Veterans of the microdot. Agents of the filing cabinet. Whatever: it had all carried the same penalty.

It had been a different world, of course, and had largely vanished when the Wall came down, which was not to say there weren't still pockets of it here and there, because friends need spying on as much as enemies. But for John Bachelor's people the Active life was over, and his role was to make sure they suffered no unwelcome intrusions, no mysterious clicks on the landline; above all, that they weren't developing a tendency to broadcast the details of their lives to anyone who cared to listen. It sometimes amused Bachelor, sometimes depressed him, that he worked for the Secret Service in an era where half the population aired its private life on the web. He wasn't sure the Cold War had been preferable, but it had been more dignified.

And now his rounds were shorter by one client. That was hardly surprising – nobody on his books was younger than seventy – but what happened afterwards? When all his charges expired, what happened to John Bachelor? It was a selfish question, but it needed answering. What happened when the milk round was done? Then the door opened, and a cold blast nipped round the room. Thanks for that, he thought. He was drunk enough to read significance in the ordinary. Thanks for that.

The newcomer was Diana Taverner.

He watched her pause at the larger, noisier group and say something which roused a cheer, so probably involved money behind the bar. Then she glanced his way, or his group's way.

'Oh, God,' groaned the soak next to him. 'Here comes the ice queen.'

'She can read lips,' said Bachelor, trying not to move his own. They buzzed with the effort.

Taverner nodded at him, or perhaps at all of them, but it felt like at him. He'd been Dieter's handler. It seemed he was in for some line-managed compassion.

It was news to him that compassion was in her repertoire.

Diana Taverner – Lady Di – was one of the Park's Second Desks, and wielded much of the power around that edifice, and not a little of the glamour. In her early fifties, she wore her age more lightly than Bachelor; wore smarter outfits too. This wasn't difficult. He shifted on the bench seat; caught the end of his tie between finger and thumb, and rubbed. It felt insubstantial, somehow. When he looked up his neighbouring soak had vacated the area, and Lady Di was settling next to him.

'John.'

'. . . Diana.'

Ma'am, usually. But this was not the office.

His group had fragmented, its constituent parts repairing to the bar or the Gents, or just generally finding an excuse to be elsewhere. But this was a while seeping through Bachelor's consciousness, swaddled by alcohol as it was. He did not want to talk to Taverner, but she had at least arrived bearing more drink. He took the proffered glass gratefully, raised it to his lips, remembering at the last minute to say 'Cheers.' She didn't reply. He swallowed, set the glass down again. Tried to gauge how presentable he looked: a fool's mission. But he found himself running a hand through his hair anyway, as if that might add lustre, or bring its former colour back.

'Dieter Hess died of natural causes.' Diana Taverner's voice was always precise, but there seemed extra edge in it now. More than was called for, fuddled intuition told Bachelor, at a social occasion. 'Just thought you'd like to know.'

It hadn't occurred to him there'd be any other explanation.

'He'd been sick for a while,' he said. 'Was on medication. Heart pills.'

'Do you remember what?'

Of course he didn't remember what. Wouldn't remember sober, couldn't remember drunk. 'Xeno-cyclitron?' he freewheeled. 'Or something like.'

She stared.

I did say 'or something like', he thought.

'When was the last time you saw him?'

'Alive?'

'Of course alive.'

'Well then.' He gathered thoughts. 'That would be last Tuesday. I spent the afternoon with him, chatting. Or listening, mostly. He complained a lot. Well, they all do.' He added this to avoid accusations of speaking ill of the dead. Speak ill of the whole bunch of them, and the dead don't feel singled out.

'Money?'

'Always money. They never have enough. Prices rising, and their income's fixed . . . I mean, is it just me, or do you ever think, it's not like they have mortgages to pay? I know they've done their bit and all, but . . .'

Even drunk, Bachelor wasn't sure he was putting his argument cogently. Also, he felt he might be coming across mean-spirited.

'Well,' he amended. 'Of course they've done their bit. That's why we're looking after them, right?'

He reached for his glass.

When he looked at Taverner again, her face was cold.

'He complained about money,' she said.

'Yes. But they all do. Did. I mean, they still do, but he—'

'So he didn't mention an alternative source of income?'

Sobriety had never been so swift nor so unwelcome.

He said, 'Ah. No. I mean . . .' He stopped. His tongue had swollen to twice its size, and sucked up his mouth's moisture.

'Strange that he'd keep that quiet, don't you think?'

'What happened?'

'You were his handler, John,' she reminded him. 'That doesn't just mean making sure he's fed and watered, and listening to his grouses. It means checking his hide for fleas. You—'

'What happened?'

He'd just interrupted Diana Taverner in full flow. Better men had been sandblasted for less.

'Dieter had a bank account you didn't know about.'

'Oh Christ.'

'And there was money going into it. Not sure where from yet, because someone's gone to a lot of trouble to hide the source. But that in itself is somewhat suggestive, wouldn't you say?'

He was going to be sick. He could feel the heave gathering force. He was going to be sick. He was going to be sick.

He'd finished his drink.

Diana Taverner regarded him the way a crow regards carrion. Eventually, she picked up her glass. Bachelor craved that glass. He'd kill for its contents. He had to settle for watching her swallow from it.

She said, 'It's hardly *Tinker, Tailor*, John. You wipe their noses, feed their cats, make sure they're not blowing their pensions on internet poker, and – and I really didn't think this needed emphasising – and above all, make sure they don't have bank accounts they're not telling us about. You want to take a guess as to why that's so important?'

He mumbled something about being compromised.

'That's right, John. Because if they've got secret bank accounts someone else is filling with money, it might mean they've been compromised. You know, I'm going to go out on a limb here. It very definitely certainly fucking does mean they've been compromised, which means we can't trust anything they've ever told us, and do you have any idea, John, do you have the remotest idea of the headache that'll cause? When we have to go trawling through everything we ever thought we knew about everything they ever told us? To find out where the lies start, and what actions we took based on them?'

'Ancient history,' he found himself saying.

'That's right, John. Ancient history. Like discovering your house's foundations aren't made of stone but pizza dough, but what's the harm, right? Now go get me another one of these.'

He did what he was told, each action muffled by a sense of impending doom. The floor buckled beneath his feet. Laughter boomed from the youngsters' table, and he knew it was aimed at him. He paid for three doubles, downed the first, and carried the survivors back to land.

Look for a loophole, he screamed inwardly. Just because this is happening doesn't mean it can't be unhappened. He was fifty-six years old. He didn't have much of a career, but he didn't have anything else going for him.

Setting her drink in front of Lady Di, he asked, 'How long?'

'More than two years.'

'How much?'

'Eighteen grand. Give or take.'

He said, 'Well, that's not—'

She raised a hand. He shut his mouth.

For a few minutes, they sat in silence. It was almost peaceful. If this could go on forever – if there never had to be a moment when the consequences of Dieter Hess receiving money from unknown sources had to be faced – then he could live with it. Stay on this seat in this pub, with this full glass in front of him, and the future forever unreached. Except that the future was already nibbling away, because look, see, his glass, it was emptying.

At last, and possibly because she was reading his mind, Taverner said, 'How old are you, John?'

It wasn't a question you asked because you wanted to know the answer. It was a question you asked because you wanted to crush your underling underfoot.

He said, 'Just tell me the worst, would you? What is it, Slough House? I'll be sent to join the other screw-ups?'

'Not everyone who screws up gets to join the slow horses. Only those it'd be impolitic to sack. That clear enough for you?'

That was clear enough for him.

'Dieter was an asset,' she went on. 'And assets, even retired assets, even *dead* assets, fall on my desk. Which means I do not want the Dogs sniffing round this, because it makes me look bad.'

The Dogs were the Service's police.

'And what makes me look bad makes you look redundant.'

Her eyes had never left his during this speech.

He was starting to get an inkling of how mice felt, and other little jungle residents. The kind preyed on by snakes.

'So. How do you think we resolve this situation?'

He shook his head.

'Excellent. And there's the can-do attitude that's made your career such a shining example to us all.' She leaned forward. 'If this gets to be an inquiry, John, you won't just be out on your ear, you'll be implicated in whatever crap Dieter Hess was up to. I'll make sure of that. And we're not just talking loss of job, John, we're talking loss of pension. Loss of any kind of benefit whatsoever. The best your future holds is a job in a supermarket, assuming you're still of working age when they let you out of prison. Just stop me when you come up with a plan. Not stopping me yet? It isn't looking good, John, is it? Not looking good at all.'

He found his voice. 'I can fix this.'

'Really? How very very marvellous.'

'I'll find out what he was doing. Put it right.'

'Then I suggest you start immediately. Because that's how soon I'll expect to be hearing from you.'

She put her glass down.

'Are you still here?'

He made it to the street somehow, where he went stumbling for the nearest lamppost, grabbed it like a sailor grabs a mast, and puked into the gutter, all the evening's drink pouring out of him in one ugly flood.

Across the road, a well-dressed couple averted their gaze.

It might have been the hangover, but the leakage from the headphones of the man opposite sounded like a demon's whisper. John Bachelor was on an early train to St Albans, his limbs heavy from lack of sleep, his stomach lumpy as a punchbag. Something pulsed behind his left eye and he was sure it glowed like a beacon in the gloomy carriage. The demon's whisper slithered in and out of meaning. Every time he thought he'd grasped its message, his mind greyed it out.

He had not had a good night. Good nights, anyway, were rare – at forty, Bachelor had discovered, you began dreaming of gravestones. After fifty, it was what you dreamed of when you were awake that frightened you most. Could Diana Taverner really engineer him behind bars? He wouldn't bet against it. If Dieter Hess had been in the pay of a foreign power, Bachelor would be guilty by default. Implicating him would be child's play to an old hand like Taverner.

The train flashed past a fox curled up in weeds by the side of the track, and two minutes later pulled into the station.

Bachelor stepped out into light rain, and trudged the familiar distance to Hess's flat.

For the past ten years he'd called here at least once a week. Two days earlier, letting himself in, he had known – was almost positive he'd known – that he'd be finding Dieter's body. Dieter had been sick for a while. Dieter had been an old man. And Dieter hadn't been answering Bachelor's calls – the fact was, Bachelor should have been there sooner. So the sight of Dieter at peace in his armchair, his passing eased by wine, tobacco and music, was, if anything, a relief. If he'd found Dieter face-down on the carpet, frantic scrabble marks showing his attempts to reach the phone, Bachelor would have had to work the scene a little, cover up any appearance of neglect. He'd been Dieter's handler, as Taverner had kept reminding him. Letting his charges die alone in pain didn't look good.

Any more than having them turn out doubles did.

But it was too soon to say whether Dieter had been a double. There were other explanations, other possibilities, for Dieter having had an illicit source of income. All Bachelor had to do was find one.

The flat had been searched, as protocol demanded, but not torn apart – the significance of the paperwork removed from Dieter's desk had only come to light back at the Park. What John Bachelor embarked on now was more thorough. He began in the kitchen, and after spreading newspaper on the floor he went through cupboards, opening jars and dumping their contents onto the paper; reading the entrails of Dieter's groceries, and finding nothing that shed light on his own future or on Dieter's past. All that came to light were coffee grounds and teabags, and surely more jars of herbs and spices than a single man could have need of? No secrets buried under packets of sausage meat in the freezer drawers. Nothing under the sink but bottles of bleach and the usual plumbing. As he searched, Bachelor found himself working faster, intent on finishing the task in hand, and forced himself to slow down. He was breathing heavily, and on the spread-out newspaper sat a mountain of mess. He should have thought harder before launching into this. He couldn't even make himself a cup of coffee now, which would have been welcome, given the state of his head.

Bachelor closed his eyes and counted to ten. When he opened them again, nothing had improved, but he thought his heart had slowed a little. Was beating at more like its usual pace.

Think, he commanded himself. Arriving here, full of his night-time furies, he'd gone off like a Viking, which would only have made sense if Dieter had been a Viking too. But Dieter had been an old man who'd lived a careful life. A careless one would have proved much shorter. His habits of secrecy were unlikely to be laid bare by a whirlwind uprooting of the contents of his kitchen . . . *Think*.

Leaving the mess in the kitchen, he walked through the rest of the flat.

Hess's sitting room – the room in which Bachelor had found him – was the largest, occupying as much space as the others put together. Bookshelves covered three of the four walls; against the fourth, below the window and facing inwards, was Dieter's armchair. His books were the view he appreciated most, and Bachelor had spent many afternoons listening to the old man rabbit on about their contents; sessions that had reminded him of interminable childhood Sundays in the company of his grandfather, whose mind, like his shelves, was not as well stocked as Dieter's, but whose appetite for rambling on about the past was just as insatiable. At least in Dieter's case the view backwards was panoramic. He had studied history. On his shelves was collected as much of the past as he'd been able to squeeze onto them; mostly early twentieth century, and post-war too, of course. He'd once confided to Bachelor – being a handler meant hearing all sorts of secrets: romantic, political, emotional, religious; meant hearing them and passing them on – that he nursed a fantasy of finding, in all that convoluted argy-bargy of politics and revolution, pogrom and upheaval, the key error; the single moment that could be retrospectively undone, and all the messiness of modern Europe set to rights. In Dieter's perfect world, he'd have stayed the German he was born. East and west would have been directions on a map.

Borderline obsessive, had been the verdict from the Park. But then, if your retired assets weren't borderline obsessive, they'd never have been assets in the first place.

There was poetry too, and fiction in a segregated corner, but Hess's taste in that area had been stern. He'd admired Flaubert above all writers, but had a compulsion to arrange, and rearrange, the great Russians in order of merit, as if the bulky tomes were jostling for a place in the starting line-up. Just looking at these novels' width aggravated Bachelor's headache. Their colours were as dull as their contents threatened, but a cheekier red-and-white spine nestled among its beefy brothers and sisters proved to be a paperback of Robert Harris's *Fatherland*. He wondered if that, too, had offered a glimpse of a happier twentieth century for Dieter Hess. One in which the war had fallen to the other side.

He moved on. The flat was near the railway line, and from the bathroom window could be seen trains heading for London and deeper into the commuter belt. It was a sash window and the wood had rotted round the edges of the frame, and its white paint flaked at the touch. It was about a year past the point Dieter should have had something done about it, just as the carpet – fraying around the rods holding it in place at the bathroom and kitchen doorways – was beyond shabby and edging into hazard country. It wasn't a big flat. If you tripped in a doorway, your head was going to hit something – the bath, the cooker – on its way down. Bachelor supposed he should have pointed this out back when it was likely to do some good, but the way things turned out, it hadn't mattered. He opened the bathroom cabinet, then closed it again. He wasn't looking for anything hidden in plain view.

The bedroom was small, with a single bed, and a wardrobe full of old-man shirts on wire hangers, their collars frayed. A faint smell he couldn't put a finger on brought hospitals to mind. The window overlooked the front street, and was near enough to a lamppost for the light to have been a bother. More books were stacked in piles along one wall. On a chest of drawers sat a hairbrush still clogged with old-man hair. Bachelor shuddered, as if something with a heavy tread had stomped across his future. Except even this, even this much, was going to look pretty desirable if he wound up paying the price for Dieter's secret life.

It was all neat enough. Everything where it was supposed to be. What if the only things hidden were hidden inside Dieter's head? What if there were no clues, no evidence, and the bank account was nothing more than his own savings, channelled through various offshore havens in order to, whatever, hide it from the taxman? But would Dieter have known how to do that? He'd been a bureaucrat. He'd known how to open a filing cabinet and use a dead-letter drop, and even that much had been decades ago. Money laundering would have been a whole new venture, and why would he be laundering his own money anyway? Bachelor was grasping at twigs, and knew it. He needed to stop the panicky theorising and get to work.

He was there for hours. He started again in the bathroom, prising the cabinet off the wall and shining a torch into the corners of the airing cupboard. In the bedroom he upturned the furniture and ran a hand round the skirting board, checking for hidden compartments. He worked the bookshelves, because he had no alternative, opening book after book, holding them by the spines and shaking, half-expecting after the first few hundred that words would start floating loose; that he'd drown in alphabet soup. Halfway done he gave up and returned to the kitchen, stepped around the mess he'd made and put the kettle on, then had to rescue an untorn teabag from the pile. He drank the unsatisfactory cuppa upright, leaning against the kitchen wall, glaring at the fraying ends of the carpet where it met the rod at the doorway. And then, because he couldn't face returning to the unending bookshelves, he knelt and prised the rod up. It came away easily, as if used to such treatment, and one of its screws dropped onto the lino and rolled under the fridge. Setting the rod aside he raised the carpet. Below it was an even thinner, disintegrating underlay, part of which came away in Bachelor's hand as he tugged.

In the exposed gap, so obviously waiting for him it might as well have been addressed, lay a plain white envelope.

In a pub on a nearby corner, Bachelor took stock. It was early doors, and he was first there, so he spread the contents of the envelope on his table as he supped a pint of bitter and felt his hangover recede slightly, to be replaced by something larger, and worse. If he'd hoped for an innocent explanation for Dieter's secret bank account, these papers put the kibosh on that. Dieter hadn't been innocent. Dieter had been hiding something. Had hidden it not only in an envelope beneath his carpet, but in code.

3/81.

4/19.

5/26.

And so on . . .

There were two pages of this, the numbers grouped in random sequences: four on one line, seven on the following, and so on. Twenty lines in all. Typed, they'd have taken up less than half a sheet, but Dieter Hess had been old school, and Dieter Hess didn't own a typewriter let alone a computer. And what this was was old-school code, a book cipher. They still taught book ciphers to newbies, in the same way they still taught Morse, the idea being that when it all went to pot, the old values would see you through. A book cipher was unbreakable without the book in front of you. Alan Turing would have been reduced to guesswork. Because there were no repetitions, no reliable frequencies hinting that *this* meant E and *that* was a T or an S. All you had were reference points. Without the book they were drawn from you were not only paddleless, you didn't have a canoe. And one thing Dieter had had in abundance was books

– with all that raw material on his shelves, he could have constructed a whole new language, let alone a Boy-Scout code. An impossible task, thought Bachelor. Impossible. No sensible place to begin.

Then he took the old man's copy of *Fatherland* from his pocket, and deciphered the list.

Two pints later, he was on the train heading back into London. It was mostly empty, but he could still hear that demonic whisper – maybe it was Dieter. Maybe he was haunted by Dieter Hess.

The list had been precisely that: a list. A list of names, none of which meant anything to Bachelor. Four women, six men: Mary Ableman to Hannah Weiss; Eric Goulding to Paul Tennant. *Dum de dum de dum de dum*. Just thinking them, they took on the rhythm of the railway. Why had Dieter copied them out, hidden them under his carpet? Because it was a crib sheet, Bachelor answered himself. Whoever these people were, Dieter had referred to them often in whatever coded messages he had sent, ciphered letters painstakingly printed in his large looping hand. To save reciphering them every time, he'd copied out this list. It wasn't Moscow rules – was shocking tradecraft – but to be fair to Dieter, he'd grown old and died before anybody stumbled on his lapse.

Dum de dum de dum de dum. It was the sound of Bachelor's own execution growing nearer. He'd gone to find proof of Dieter's innocence. What he had in his pocket proved the bastard's guilt: he'd been writing, often enough that he needed a crib sheet, to someone with a paperback of *Fatherland* to hand – *3/81* = third page, eighty-first character = M; *4/19* = A; *5/26* = R; *6/18* = Y, and so on, and so very bloody forth . . . Lady Di would have him flayed alive. Just knowing there were names being bandied round in code: she'd have him peeled and eaten by fish. And God only knew what she'd come up with if it turned out these coded characters were up to *mischief.*

He could abscond, the three pints of bitter suggested. He could flit home, grab his getaway kit – passport and a few appearance-adjusting tools, including fake glasses and a shoe-insert, to give him a limp: heaven help him – but even if the bitter had been convincing, the plan fell apart at the first hurdle, which was made of money. Divorce had cleaned him out, and it had been years since his escape kit had included the couple of grand that was the bare minimum for a disappearing trick. And it was one thing imagining himself a stylish expat in Lisbon, admiring the sunshine from a café on the quay; quite another to picture the probable reality: hanging round bus stations, begging for loose change.

Besides, even if he'd had the money, did he any longer have the nerve? The view through the windows was dreary, a grey parade of unidentifiable crops in boring fields, soon to be replaced by the equally unappetising back-ends of houses, with flags of St George hanging limply from upstairs windows, and mildewed trampolines leaning against fences – but it was where he belonged. Everyone needs somewhere to imagine escaping from, which didn't mean they wanted to leave it for good. Those young-man dreams of living each day as if it were your last, they wore off; showed up, in the cold light of after-fifty, for the magpie treasures they were. Live every day as if it were your last. So come nightfall, you'd have no job, no savings, and be bloody miles away. He wanted to stay where he was. He wanted his job to continue, his pension to remain secure. His life to continue unruffled.

Which meant he had to do something about this list before Lady Di got her hands on it.

He could destroy it, but if he did that before unravelling its meaning, he might be storing up grief to come. That was the trouble with the spying game: there were too many imponderables. But a list of names that meant nothing . . . He wouldn't know where to start.

The train ploughed on, and fields gave way to houses. Even after it came to a halt, Bachelor remained in his seat, watching without seeing the half-busy platforms. At length, he stood. He had a plan. It wasn't much of a plan, and involved a lot of luck and twice as much bullshit, but it was the best he could do at short notice.

And let's face it, he told himself as he headed for the Underground, you've been coasting for

years. If there's any spook left in you, let's see if
he can pull this off.

Bachelor was headed across the river. This wasn't
as bad as it sounded. In a profession whose every
activity came encrypted in jargon, this one was
happily literal, and didn't betoken an over-the-
Styx moment, or not yet it didn't.

Some who worked there might have taken issue
with this. The office complex from which various
Service departments operated – Background, Psych
Eval and Identities, among others – was far removed
from the dignity of Regent's Park, and a sense of
second-class citizenry permeated its walls. Had it
been *just* across the river – had it enjoyed a water-
side view, for instance – things might have been
different, but in this case over the river meant quite
some distance over; far enough to leave its more
ambitious inhabitants feeling they'd bought a loser's
ticket in the postcode lottery. Nevertheless, the
phrase was geographical, not metaphorical, which
meant that those working across the river were in
better shape, linguistically and otherwise, than the

denizens of Slough House, which wasn't in Slough, wasn't a house, and was where screw-up spooks were sent to make them wish they'd died.

But not everyone who screws up gets to join the slow horses. Only those it'd be impolitic to sack . . .

He'd made calls, discovered who the newbies were. In an organisation this size there was always someone who'd just walked through the door, and while the training they'd been put through was more intense than most office jobs demanded, they'd still be the easiest pickings. With three names in his head, he checked their current whereabouts with security: showing his pass, barking his requests, to forestall any inquisition into his motives. Two of the newbies were out of the building. The third, J. K. Coe, was hot-desking on the fourth floor, not having been assigned a permanent workstation yet.

'Thanks,' Bachelor said. His card had been logged on entry, and for all he knew this exchange had been recorded, but he'd come up with something plausible, or at least not outrageous, to use if he were quizzed. *Coe. Thought I'd known his father. Turned out to be a different branch.*

Coe, when Bachelor tracked him down, looked to be early thirties or thereabouts, which was old for a recruit, but not as unusual as it had once been. 'Hinterland' was a buzzword now; it was good to have recruits with hinterland, because, well, it just was – Bachelor had forgotten the argument, if he'd even been listening when he'd heard it. Somehow, the Service had evolved into the kind of organisation which most of its recruits had joined it to avoid, but that was a rant for another day. Coe, anyway: early thirties. His particular hinterland lay in the City; he'd been in banking until the profession had turned toxic, but his degree had been in psychology.

'You're Coe?'

The young man's eyes were guarded. Bachelor didn't blame him. The first few weeks in any job, you had to be on your mettle. In the Service, that went times a hundred. Most unscheduled events were official mind games – googlies bowled at newbies, to see how they'd stand up under pressure – and some were co-workers' mind-fucks, to see whether the virgin had a sense of humour. Depending on the department, this meant laughing off anything from a debagging to life-threatening harm, to show you weren't a spoilsport.

All or most of which probably went through J. K. Coe's head before he replied.

'Yes.'

'Bachelor. John.' He showed Coe his ID, which was about twenty-five generations older than Coe's own. 'You're through with induction, right?'

'Yesterday.'

'Good. I've a job for you.'

'And you're . . .'

'From the Park. I work with Diana Taverner.'

And there was the word *with* stretched far as it would go; way beyond where it might snap back in his face and lay him open to the bone.

From his pocket, he produced a sealed envelope containing the deciphered list of names. Before handing it over, he scribbled Coe's own name on the front.

'I want background on each of them, including current whereabouts. "All significant activities" – is that still the phrase you're taught?'

'Yes, but—'

'Good, because that's what I want to hear about. All significant activities, meaning jobs, contacts, travels abroad. But I don't need to tell you your job, do I?'

'You kind of do,' said Coe.

'You work here, right?'

'Psych Eval. I'm putting together a questionnaire for new recruits? Even newer ones, I mean.'

A sheepish smile went with this.

'Maybe you'd like to call Lady Di, then. Explain why you're knocking her back.' Bachelor produced his mobile. 'I can give you her direct line.'

'All I meant, no, nothing. Sure. Here.' Coe took the envelope. 'Am I looking for anything . . . in particular?'

'Information, Coe. Data. Background.' Bachelor leaned forward, conspiratorially. The cubicle he'd found Coe in was surrounded by vacant workstations, but it was always worth making the effort. 'In fact, let's say that what you've got here's a network. Deep cover. And you're looking to prove it. Ten ordinary people, and what you're after is the connection, the thread that links them. Which could be – well, you don't need me to tell you. It could be anything.'

Coe's eyes had taken on a vague cast, which on a civilian might mean he was tuning out. Bachelor assumed it here meant the opposite; that Coe was drawing up a mental schedule: where he'd start, what channels he'd take. Analysts, in Bachelor's experience, were always drawing mental maps.

He wondered whether he should stress how confidential this was, but decided not to rouse the newby's suspicions. Besides, how stupid would Coe have to be to go blabbing to all and sundry?

He said, 'The good news is, you've got a whole twenty-four hours.'

'Is this live?' Coe asked. 'I mean, is this an actual op?'

Bachelor touched a finger to his lips.

'Jesus,' Coe said. He glanced around, but there was nobody in sight. 'That long?'

'Banks shut at four-thirty, don't they? News flash. You don't work in a bank any more.'

'It wasn't that kind of banking,' Coe said. He glanced at the list in his hand, then back at Bachelor. 'Where do I bring the product?'

'My number's on the sheet. Call me. Do this right, and you've a friend in Regent's Park.'

'Who works with Diana Taverner,' said Coe.

'Closely. Who works *closely* with Diana Taverner.'

'Yes. I've heard she picks favourites.'

Bachelor wondered if he'd made the right choice, a psych grad, but it was too late now.

Coe said, 'I spent a night in a ditch last month, in freezing fog. Out on the Stiperstones?'

Bachelor knew the Stiperstones.

'I was told it was part of a reconnaissance exercise. Counted towards my pass rate. Turned out it was a wind-up. Left me so shagged out I nearly failed the next day's module.'

Bachelor said, 'We've all been there. What's your point?'

Coe looked like he had a point, and it was no doubt something to do with the kind of emotions he'd feel, or the sort of vengeance he'd hope to wreak, if it turned out that Bachelor had just handed him the desk-bound equivalent of a night in a freezing ditch.

'. . . Nothing.'

'Good man. We'll speak tomorrow.'

Bachelor left the building still with the ghost of a hangover scratching his skull. Maybe Coe would come up with something he could shield himself with when Lady Di made her next move. More likely this was a waste of time, but time was currently the only thing he had on his calendar.

It might help.

It probably wouldn't hurt.

It depended on how good J. K. Coe was.

How good J. K. Coe was was something J. K. Coe had been wondering himself. The complex knot of his reasons for joining the Service had tightened in his mind to the extent that rather than attempt untangling them, it was simpler to slice right through. On one side fell disillusionment with the banking profession; on the other, an interview he'd read in a Canary Wharf giveaway magazine with an intelligence services' recruitment officer. Like any boy, he'd once harboured fantasies of being a spy. The fact that here in grown-up life, the opportunity actually existed – that there was a number you could ring! – offered a glimmer of light in what had become, far sooner than he'd been expecting, a wearisome way of making a living.

It turned out that a psychology degree and a background in investment banking fitted Five's profile of desirable candidates. That's what Coe had been told, anyway. It was possible they said that sort of thing a lot.

But here he was now, less than a week into fledgling status, and he'd been handed what had looked like a desk job but was rapidly becoming more intriguing. It might be, of course, that this was another set-up, and that Bachelor – if that was really his name – was even now celebrating Coe's gullibility in a nearby pub, but still: if this was a time-wasting riddle, it appeared to be one with an answer, even if that remained for the moment ungraspable as smoke.

Because the names he'd been given belonged to real people. Using the Background database, for which Coe had only ground-level clearance, but which nevertheless gave access to a lot of major record sets – utilities, census, vehicle and media licensing, health and benefits data, and all the other inescapable ways footprints are left in the social clay – he'd established possible identities for each name on Bachelor's list, and caught a glimmer, too, of a connecting thread. He thought of this in terms of a spider's web in a hedge: one moment it's there, in all its complicated functionality; the next, when you shift your perspective an inch, it's gone.

There were real people with these names, but if they made up a network, it can't have been a terribly effective one. Because almost all of them were lock-aways of one sort or another. Care homes, hospitals, prison . . . Each time he tilted his head, the perspective shifted.

The afternoon had swum away, leaching all light from the sky. Coe hadn't eaten since mid-morning, a bacon sandwich he'd been planning to trade off against lunch, but he hadn't reckoned on skipping supper too. He should call a halt now, but if he did, there was no telling he'd get any further with his task in the morning; odds-on he'd be called to account for that questionnaire he'd barely started. And this was more interesting than devising trip-up questions, and now he had his teeth in, he didn't want to let go . . .

But he needed help. Oddly, he had an idea where it might be found.

A lecture he'd attended the previous month had been given by a Regent's Park records officer. She ran a whole floor, it was whispered; ran it like a dragon runs its lair, and it was easy to see how the dragon rumour started, because she was a fearsome lady. Wheelchair-bound, with a general demeanour that just dared you to give a shit about it, she'd held her audience if not spellbound then certainly gobsmacked, through the simple expedient of giving the first student she caught drifting such a bollocking he probably still trembled when reminded of it now. In one fell swoop, the drag-on-lady had resurrected several dozen bad school memories. She'd quickly been dubbed Voldemort.

Funny thing was, J. K. Coe had rather liked Molly Doran, who was every bit as round as she was legless, and powdered her face so thickly she might have been a circus turn. Her lecture – on information collation in a pre-digital era: *not*, she emphasised, an historical curiosity, but an in-the-field survival technique – had been brisk and intelligent, and when she'd finished by announcing that she would not be taking questions because she'd already answered any they might be capable of coming up with, it had been with the air of delivering a tiresome truth rather than playing for laughs. She had added, though, that she expected to see the more intelligent among them again, because sooner or later the more gifted would need her help.

Only J. K. Coe had offered the traditional round of applause once she was done, and he quit after two claps when it was clear he was on his own. He'd been relieved Doran had had her back to the class, shuffling her papers into a bag, and hadn't seen him.

Two thumbs down from his classmates then, but that was okay. Coe, the oldest in his recruitment wave, felt licensed to divert from the popular opinion. Molly Doran was – no getting round this – a 'character', and having escaped a profession which prided itself on its characters, this being how it labelled those who read *The Art of War* on the Tube, Coe was gratified to have come across the real thing. Already he'd heard two conflicting stories behind the loss of Doran's legs, and this too was a source of pleasure. The Service thrived on legends.

He could track down people with the bare minimum to go on, he'd proved that much today. It wasn't a stretch coming up with Molly Doran's extension number; nor was it a surprise that she was still within reach of it, down in the bowels of the Park, on the right side of the river.

Legends don't keep office hours.

Coe explained who he was.

She said, 'You're the one who clapped, aren't you?'

He could see his reflection in his monitor as he heard the words, and afterwards had the strange sensation that his reflection had been observing his reaction, rather than the other way round. Certainly, it seemed to retain an unusual state of calm for one who'd just been presented with evidence of witchcraft.

She said, 'All right, close your mouth. If you

hadn't been the one who'd clapped, you wouldn't dare call me now.'

'I'd worked that out for myself,' he lied.

She asked what he wanted, and he explained about the list; not saying where he'd got it from, just that it was a puzzle he'd been presented with. Besides, he reasoned, Bachelor hadn't sworn him to secrecy.

'And what do you expect from me?'

'Something you said in your lecture,' Coe said. 'You said don't muck about with secondary sources—'

'I said *what*?'

'– You said don't fuck about with secondary sources if there's a primary available. And that there's always a primary available if you know where to look.'

'And I'm your primary?'

'Or you can tell me who is.'

'So you're expecting me to point you to some-one cleverer?'

'I doubt even you could manage that.'

She laughed what sounded like a smoker's laugh.

Last time he'd heard anything quite like it, he been sanding off the edge of a door.

'That's right, J. K. You did say J. K.? Not Jake?'

Some jerks get lumbered with Jason. Some saps are saddled with Kevin. But how many poor sods end up with—

'J. K.,' he confirmed.

'That's right, J. K., you ladle on the syrup. The ladies always fall for that.'

He said, 'In that case, I have to tell you, you've got a great set of wheels.'

A silence followed, during which Coe's thoughts turned to the essential elements involved in forging a new identity: fake passport, fake social security number, fake spectacles. He'd need to shave his head, too . . .

And then she was laughing again, more like a rusty bicycle chain this time.

'You little bastard,' she said.

'Sorry.'

'Don't spoil it now. You little bastard.'

He counted blessings until her laughter passed.

'So this list,' she said at last. 'This famous list.

You've found a link and you want to talk to someone who might know what it means.'

'If it is a link, and not just a coincidence—'

'Don't be boring. If you thought it was a coincidence, you'd not have called me.'

Coe said, 'They all have German connections. Some close, some not so close. But they all have connections.'

'Oh, Jesus,' Molly Doran said. 'I'm sorry, J. K.'

She sounded it, too.

'You can't help?'

'Just the opposite. I know exactly who you want to speak to.'

'Then why so sorry?'

'Ever heard of Jackson Lamb?' she asked.

In his final years as a banker, J. K. Coe had grown understandably secretive about his profession. In that sense, joining the Service hadn't involved big changes – broadcasting your daily activities was frowned upon – but he still found it hard to avoid feeling himself separate from the general sway. It was ridiculous, stupid, counter-productive – being an agent, even a back-room, across-the-river agent, meant melding in – and he knew, too, that everyone felt this way, that everyone was at the centre of their own narrative. Still, he couldn't help it. Take this trip across town right now, to talk to Jackson Lamb. Standing on the Tube, Coe was studying his fellow passengers, gauging their identities. There was a checklist he'd memorised, a cribsheet on how to spot a terrorist; and there was another checklist, allowing for the possibility that terrorists might have got hold of the first checklist and adapted their behaviour accordingly, and Coe had memorised this too. And he was mentally running through them, scoring his fellow travellers, when it struck him there was conceivably a checklist for spotting members of the security services, and he was doubtless ticking all the right boxes himself . . . The thought made him want to giggle, which itself was on one of the checklists. But he couldn't help feeling skittish. He was still in his first week, newest of newbies, and he'd shared a clubby phone call with Molly Doran, and was now on his way to meet Jackson Lamb.

Who definitely figured among the legends he'd been contemplating earlier.

Lamb was a former joe, an active undercover, who'd spent time on the other side of the Wall, back when there'd been a Wall. So he was definitely the man to talk to if you were looking for dodgy German connections stretching into the past – most of the folk on Bachelor's list were certified crumblies – but he was also someone who came trailing clouds of story, some of which had to be true. He'd been Charles Partner's golden boy once – Partner, last of the Cold War First Desks – but after Partner shot himself, Lamb had been hived off to the curious little annex called Slough House, which was right side of the river, but wrong side of the tracks. And there he'd remained ever since, presiding over his own little principality of screw-ups. Some of the stories said he'd been a genius spy; others that he'd blown a whole network, and was the only one who'd come back alive. Nobody Coe knew had ever laid eyes on him. Well, nobody except Molly Doran, and he couldn't really claim to know her.

He'd phoned Slough House and spoken to a

woman called Standish. When he'd said he wanted to speak to Lamb, she seemed to be waiting for the punchline. So he'd explained about the list, and she'd told him Lamb didn't talk to strangers on the phone, and wasn't terribly likely to speak to him in person. But if he was prepared to head over Barbican way, she'd see what she could do.

What she could do involved opening the door for him. This was round the back, as she'd said on the phone: Slough House had a front door, but it hadn't been used in so long, she couldn't guarantee it actually worked. 'Round the back' was via a mildew-coated yard. There was no light, and Coe barked his shin on something unidentifiable, so was leaning against the door grimacing when it opened, and he came this close to measuring his length in a dank hallway.

'Now there's an entrance,' the woman said.

'Sorry. That yard's a deathtrap.'

'We don't get many visitors. Come on. He's on the top floor.'

Trooping up the stairs felt like ascending to Sweeney Todd's lair. Coe didn't know what that made Catherine Standish, who'd have been a dead ringer for a woman in white – a lady with a lamp – had she worn white, or carried a lamp. But her long-sleeved dress had ruffled sleeves, and Coe believed he caught a glimpse of petticoat in the two-inch gap between its hem and the strap of her shoe. But Slough House, Jesus . . . Regent's Park was impressive – a cross between old world class and hi-tech flash – and his own across-the-river complex, if drab, was functional, and had been gutted and refitted often enough that you sensed an attempt to keep up with the times. But Slough House was time-warped, a little patch of seventies' squalor, with peeling walls and creaking stairs. The bare lightbulbs highlit patches of damp that resembled large-scale maps, as if the staircase had been designed by a wheezing cartographer. And in the corners of the stairs lurked dustballs so big they might have been nests. He wasn't sure whose nests. Didn't want to be.

On each landing a pair of office doors stood open. They were vacant and unlit, and drifting from their gloomy shadows came a mixture of odours

Coe couldn't help adumbrating: coffee and stale bread, and takeaway food, and cardboard, and grief.

He thought something moved.

'Did I just see a cat?'

'No.'

And up they went, up to the top floor, and a small hallway with office doors facing each other from either side. One stood open, and was lit by a couple of standard lamps; the effect wasn't exactly cosy – it remained a drably furnished office – but at least it looked like a space in which things got done. This was Standish's own, Coe assumed. Which meant that the other—

'You'd better knock.'

He did.

'Who the hell's that?'

'Good luck,' said Catherine Standish, and disappeared into her room, closing the door behind her.

Okay, so Coe was about to meet a Service legend. *Beard him in his den* was the phrase that came unbidden, and he raised his hand to knock again, this time while announcing his name in a pleasing, manly fashion, when the door opened without warning.

So here was Jackson Lamb.

He didn't look like a legend. He looked like a Punch cartoon of a drunk artist, in a jacket that might have been corduroy once, and another colour – it was currently brown – over a collar-less white shirt. What a kinder observer might call a cravat hung round his neck, and his hair was yellowy-grey, with clumps sticking out at odd angles. More hair, much darker, could be seen poking through his shirt at stomach level. As for his face, this was rounded and jowly and blotchy; there was a slight gap between his two front teeth, visible below a snarling lip. Yes, like a caricature of an artist, and one in the grip of some creative urge or other. His eyes were heavy with suspicion.

'Who are you?'

'Ah, J. K. Coe—'

'Oh Christ. I've told her about letting strays in. What are you selling?'

'I'm not selling anything.'

Lamb grunted. 'Everybody's selling something.'

He withdrew into his room, and since he did so without actually telling Coe to get lost, Coe followed.

The room's sole illumination was a lamp set upon a pile of books, which on second glance turned out to be telephone directories. In the feeble yellow light it cast, Coe could make out a desk whose most prominent ornaments were a bottle of whisky and a pair of shoes. In the shadows round the walls lurked what Coe took for filing cabinets and shelves. Blinds were drawn over the sole window, but a cracked blade hung loose, and through the gap some of the evening's dark leaked into the room, offset by tiny reflections of the traffic on Aldersgate Street, blinking in the beads of moisture hanging on the glass.

Lamb didn't so much settle into his chair as collapse into it. The noise it greeted him with was one of resigned discomfort.

'You're from over the river,' Lamb said, reaching for the bottle.

'Ms Standish told you?'

'Do I look like I've time to gossip? She didn't

even tell me you were coming. But you're hardly from the Park, are you? Not unless they've widened their entry criteria.' Looking up, he added, 'It's a class thing. Don't worry about it.'

'Lamb is easily bored,' Molly Doran had said. 'Play him right, and he'll bend your ear for hours. But if he's in one of his moods, forget it.'

'But this is work,' Coe had said. 'It's Service business.'

'That's sweet. I remember my first week.' Doran paused. 'Oh, and one other thing. Don't tell him I sent you. Got it?'

'Got it.'

So here, in place of the truth, was Coe's reason for approaching Lamb:

'Everyone says you're the one to talk to.'

'Everyone says that, do they?'

'You lived the life. Ran your own network, survived for years. They say—'

Lamb interrupted with a fart, then said in a plummy tone, 'I do apologise. That's never happened before.'

Coe said, 'They say you were the best.'

53

'I was, was I?'

'And my problem's about a network . . .'

He paused. He seemed to be always pausing. This time, he was partly waiting for permission to continue; partly wondering if Lamb was ever going to invite him to sit. But there was nowhere obvious to sit that didn't involve retreating into the shadows, and while he didn't actually believe anything untoward lurked by the walls, he was a little concerned about the floorboards. The air of rot was more pronounced than it had been on the stairs. He figured he was okay if he remained in the middle of the room.

Lamb had closed his eyes, and linked his fingers across his paunch. His feet were visible on Coe's side of the desk, and he was indeed shoeless, which perhaps accounted for some small part of the atmosphere. Lamb's recent emission hadn't helped. He grunted now, and when this didn't spur Coe on, opened an eye. 'You don't need to tell me about your problem, son. I already know what your problem is.'

So Doran had called him after all, Coe thought.

He realised he was caught in the middle of some complicated game between this man and Molly Doran, as intricate as any courtship ritual, but that didn't matter now, because the important thing was, Lamb was going to explain the oddities in this supposed network . . .

'Your problem is, you're lying. Nobody talks about me on the other side of the river, or when they do, it's not to say how brilliant I am. It's to say I'm a fat old bastard who should have been put out to grass long ago.'

'I—'

'And it's not only the lying. You'll never get anywhere in this business without lying. No, your problem's twofold. First off, as you've probably worked out for yourself already, you're no good at it.'

'I was told not to tell you—'

'And second, it's me you're lying to.'

All of this with just one eye open, trained on Coe. It was extraordinary, thought Coe, how much a badly dressed shoeless fat man could look like a crocodile.

'And you've no idea how cross I get when that happens.'

But he was about to find out.

It was after nine when Catherine Standish entered Lamb's room again. Lamb was in his chair, eyes closed, shoeless feet propped on his wastepaper bin. A bottle of Talisker sat on his desk, a pair of thumb-greased glasses next to it. One was a quarter full, or possibly three quarters empty. The other, while not exactly clean, was at least unused.

She knew the routine, a recent parlour game of Lamb's. No point talking until she poured herself a glass. This was what passed, in his mind, for good-natured teasing.

Slough House had been empty of staff for hours, the pair of them apart. For Catherine there was always work to do, a neverending cascade of it. For Lamb, she sometimes thought, there was nowhere else to be. He had a home; might even – now here was a thought – have a family some-where. She thought that less likely than finding intelligent life on Twitter, but still: there had to be a reason he spent so many of his waking hours here, even if a goodly fraction of those waking hours were spent asleep.

Without touching the glass she poured a slug of whisky into it, then added a pile of newspapers from the visitor's chair to the bigger pile on the floor next to it, and sat.

She said, 'That wasn't very helpful.'

He didn't open his eyes. 'This is me you're talking to?'

'We're all part of the Service. So someone thought it would be funny to send a Daniel into your den. That doesn't mean he didn't need real information.'

'I didn't object to the little bastard turning up. I objected to the little bastard trying to play me.'

'Well, I think we can safely say he won't try that again.'

J. K. Coe's departure had been precipitous, making up in speed what it lacked in dignity.

'Did you know him?'

'He's still in his first week. Refugee from banking, but he scored high on the entrance exams and—'

'Entrance exams,' said Lamb. 'God help us.'

'I know,' Catherine said. 'Just give them a Double-Oh-Seven watch and drop them behind enemy lines. Never did you any harm.'

'Well, we can't all be me,' Lamb said reasonably. 'What's his day job?'

'Psych Eval.'

'For a washed-up alky, you're still plugged into the network, aren't you?'

Washed-up was right. Catherine's career, like a castaway's message, had been sealed inside a bottle and tossed overboard. Slough House was where it had beached, and in the years since she hadn't touched a drop.

The amount of booze Lamb had put away in that time would float a hippo.

'It's funny,' she said. 'I'm sitting here dry as a bone while you souse yourself nightly. How come I'm a drunk and you're not?'

'Drunks have blackouts,' he explained kindly. 'And wake up in strangers' beds. I never do that.'

'When you start waking in strangers' beds, it's the strangers who ought to be worried.'

'You say tomato,' Lamb said obscurely. He reached for his glass, balanced it on his chest, and closed his eyes again. 'Tell me about the kid's problem.'

So she told him about the kid's problem. John Bachelor, one of the Park's old lags, had presented him with a list of names; find out who they are, Bachelor had said. Find out if there's a connection.

Find out if it's a network.

'Bachelor,' Lamb said without opening his eyes. 'Milkman, right?'

'He's on the milk round, yes.'

'One of his mentals just died.'

'Mentals?'

'Trust me, they're all mentals.' Lamb craned his head forward, caught the rim of his glass in his teeth, and easing his head back again, allowed the contents of the glass to pour into his mouth. He swallowed, then set the glass back on his chest. 'When Daniel Craig can do that,' he said, 'tell him to give me a ring.'

'I've made a note.'

'Dieter Hess,' Lamb continued. 'That was the bugger's name.'

'Did you know him?'

'God no. I've better things to do with my time than pal around with clapped-out spooks.'

It was true, Catherine thought, that you didn't get that adept at handless drinking without hours of practice.

'I know who he was, but not a joe, an asset. Worked in the Transport Ministry on the other side.'

When Lamb said 'the other side,' he always meant the Wall. For him, the Cold War had been geography as much as politics.

'He had access to classified info. Troop movements, that sort of thing. Fair play to him, it was useful stuff. How far did Coe get?'

Coe had done the basic searches and come up with a list of possibles connected by a thread: they all had links with Germany. They were offspring of immigrants, or had other family bonds; they had work connections; they'd studied the language and literature to degree level. In some cases, frequent holidays indicated an attachment to the country. It wasn't much, Coe had thought, but it wasn't something he was spinning out of fresh air. It was definitely there.

Lamb grunted. 'And means the list definitely came from Hess. So what's the problem?'

'The problem is, most of those on the list are shutaways. In care homes, a lot of them. Elderly. There's one who's younger, thirty-two, and he's never been anywhere else. He's severely disabled. One's been in prison for the last decade, and isn't leaving soon. Of the whole crew, there's only one at liberty, a twenty-one-year-old girl.' Lamb wasn't reacting to any of this. Hadn't even opened his eyes. 'So what Coe wants to know is, what kind of network is that?'

She leaned back in her chair and waited.

After some minutes Lamb raised his empty glass, using his hand this time. He held it in her direction. Suppressing a sigh she reached for the bottle, and filled it for him. Her own still sat where she'd left it, untouched. She was trying to pretend it wasn't there. If she looked at it by accident – if it looked back – she would turn to stone.

Lamb said, 'Any rumours on the late Hess?'

'There was money.'

'But not huge great bucketloads, right?'

'Not from what I've heard.'

And Catherine heard a lot. She had fallen far – there were those who'd argue she'd fallen further than Lamb – but the only enemy she'd made on the way was her own younger self. In her private life, she double-locked her doors. But at work she kept all channels open, and even Lamb was impressed by the range of her contacts, and their willingness to share with her.

But if she dealt in raw data, Lamb liked to build castles with it.

She said, 'You have that look.'

'What look?'

'That look where you're about to be clever, and I'm supposed to be amazed.'

Lamb belched.

'Though I could be wrong,' Catherine said.

'Coe's still slimy with afterbirth, so you can't blame him for being ignorant. But Bachelor's third-rate at best. Know him?'

'Of him.'

'Best way. All being a milkman involves is wiping noses and he can't even do that. If he asked Coe to track down these people, it's because he doesn't want to do it via channels, which means he hasn't told anyone at the Park. I expect he found the list after Hess died, and has been crapping himself in case Lady Di gets wind of it. Coe doesn't know enough to work out what it means, and he's too stupid to do it himself.'

'But you're not.'

'You probably weren't either, before you pickled what used to be your brain. You never get those cells back, do you?'

When he asked a particularly nasty question, Lamb generally required an answer.

Catherine said, 'They're usually full of information you don't want to recall anyway. If I ever struggle with your name, there's your reason.' She thought for a bit. 'The fact that it wasn't much money is a clue, isn't it?'

Lamb lit a cigarette.

She thought some more. Out on the street, a car honked and another honked back. Impossible to tell whether two friends had driven past each other, or one stranger had cut another up. There were times when it was similarly hard to tell what was happening in this room.

Hess had been receiving money to pay the people on this list. But the people weren't any kind of network; they were shut-ins and innocents.

She waved away smoke and said, 'It's a ghost network.'

'There you go. All you've ever done for the Service is type memos and boil the kettle, and even you can work it out. I despair for this generation, I really do. Bunch of Gideons.'

She didn't ask.

Not being asked never bothered Jackson Lamb. 'Talentless chancers riding on their family pull and the old school tie. Call me a hopeless idealist, but talent used to count for something.'

Catherine stood. 'Maybe we'll put that on your gravestone.'

She was halfway out the door before he said, 'You'll tell him all this, won't you?'

'Coe? Yes, I will.'

'Another lame duck. Collect as many as you like, it won't help you fly again.'

'I'm under no illusions about my future, thanks.'

'Just as well. It's not clear you have one. Unless you count this place.'

Catherine turned. 'Thanks. And by the way, what *is* that round your neck?'

'Somebody's scarf. Found it in the kitchen.' Lamb scratched the back of his neck. 'There's a draught.'

'Yes, keep it on. Don't want you catching cold.'

She went back to her own office to ring Coe, thinking: *So that's where the tea towel went.*

Lamb finished his drink, then reached for Catherine's untouched glass. A ghost network. He didn't especially approve – in Lamb's lexicon, a joe was not to be trifled with; even an imaginary joe – but the old lag had doubtless done it for beer money, which left Lamb half-inclined to applaud. A ghost network didn't require joes. All it took was a little identity theft; enough to convince your paymasters you were nurturing the real thing: verifiable names, plausibly sympathetic to whatever cause you'd hired out to. In Hess's case, he'd scraped together a crew as near their last legs as he'd been himself, but that didn't matter, because there was no way the paymasters were ever going to get an actual sniff of them. *Too soon*, he'd have said. *Too raw. Bring them on gently*. Phrases Lamb had used himself, in the long-ago, but always for real. And what were they supposed to be passing on, Hess's phantoms? Nothing major. Gossip from the corridors of power, industrial tittle-tattle, maybe hints of policy shifts; or possibly Hess had gone for something riskier, and pretended one of them was actually in the pay of the Service. Thinking about it, Lamb suspected the old boy could have made that fly. Milked John Bachelor for office gossip and passed it off as product, explaining the lack of substance everywhere else as being early yield; a thin harvest from a too-green vine, but let it grow, let it grow . . .

And it was only small sums of money.

He supped from Standish's glass. A low murmur from across the hall told him she was on the phone, giving the lowdown to Coe, who'd doubtless be puppyishly grateful, and just like that Standish had another resource to call on. Networks everywhere . . . And who could be surprised, really, that a worn-out spook had found a way to supplement his pension? Hess had been an asset, and here was a thing about assets: you could never be sure they weren't going to turn 180 degrees. Lamb accepted that now as he had done then. He hated a traitor, but defined the breed narrowly. Assets switching pavements was part of the game. Because they were the ones doing the risky business, while their paymasters risked only paper cuts.

'So no harm done,' he muttered. Least of all to John Bachelor, who'd be able to pass the whole thing off as an old man's petty larceny; if, indeed, he bothered to pass anything on at all. Ghost networks were only a problem if you believed in ghosts. Bachelor probably scraped by without that superstition.

So no, no harm done.

Unless somebody does something stupid, Lamb thought, but really, what were the chances?

★

Information is a tart – information is anybody's. It reveals as much about those who impart it as it teaches those who hear. Because information, ever the slut, swings both ways. False information – if you know it's false – tells you half as much again as the real thing, because it tells you what the other feller thinks you don't know, while real information, the copper-bottomed truth, is worth its weight in fairydust. When you have a source of real information, you ought to forsake all others and snuggle down with it for good. Even though it'll never work out, because information, first, last and always, is a tart.

This much, John Bachelor knew.

So the best thing to have, he also knew, was an asset; someone deep in the enemy's bunker – and for information purposes, everyone was an enemy – passing back knowledge that the enemy thought was his alone. But even better than that was knowing the enemy had an asset inside your own bunker, and feeding him, feeding her, information that looked like the real thing, that nobody dared to poke at, but which was false as a banker's promise.

And best of all, better than anything else, was having it both ways; was having someone the enemy only thought was their asset inside your own bunker, so while your enemy thought he was feeding you mouldy crumbs and harvesting cake, the reality was the other way round.

All of this, Bachelor wanted to explain to Di Taverner before he got on to anything else, but that wasn't going to happen. For a start, she knew it all already. And for the rest, she had other things on her mind.

'They should have taken the carpets up,' she said.

'He was an old man.'

'Your point being?'

'Nobody was expecting this. Dieter's been – had been – defunct for years. As far as anyone knew he was sitting at home reading Yeats, and drinking himself into oblivion. Cleaning up after him was a matter of respect, that's all.'

'If they'd respected him more, they'd have taken the carpets up,' she said.

They were in her office in Regent's Park, and it was mid-morning, and the artificial lighting was pretending it was spring. On her desk lay the list; Dieter Hess's coded original. The copy of *Fatherland* with which Bachelor had unwrapped its secrets sat next to it.

'And these people,' Taverner said – the people on the list – 'they're all real?'

'They exist, but they're not a network.' He'd told her this already, but it was important to emphasise the point: that Dieter Hess had not – had *not* – been running a coy little op behind Bachelor's back, but had simply been filching pennies to ease his days; to pay for his wine and his books; to ensure, God help us all, that he could turn the heating up. So Bachelor laid it out again, this information that had seeped down from Jackson Lamb to Catherine Standish; from Standish to J. K. Coe; from Coe to John Bachelor, and was even now being soaked up by Diana Taverner: that the people whose encoded names had been laboriously printed on that sheet of paper in most cases probably didn't know what day of the week it was, let alone that they were spies. Dieter Hess had picked their pockets, though all he had taken was their names.

'Why them in particular?'

'For their German links. He needed people the BND would believe in.'

The Bundesnachrichtendienst was the German intelligence service.

'Do me the smallest of favours and don't treat me like an idiot. I meant why people in homes, in hospitals? Out of circulation?'

'Safer. He didn't want anyone who was going to make waves. You know, win the lottery or something. Get in the papers. Draw attention.'

'Then what about the younger one? Why doesn't she fit the pattern?'

'He wanted a live one. Obviously.'

Her eyes flashed danger. 'What's obvious about it?'

'I didn't mean obvious, I just meant I've been thinking about it.' Jesus. 'He wanted someone he could demonstrate was live and kicking, if he needed to.'

'Like when? How did this scam work? If it was a scam. The jury's still out.'

'It worked on old-school principles,' Bachelor

said. 'The kind that mean, if you've got an agent in place, you don't put them on parade. Hess was known to the BND, of course he was. He defected, after all. Ancient history, but still. So if he claimed, I don't know, regret, or willingness to make amends now the Fatherland's reunited, he'd have found a willing ear. He was a persuasive man. That's how he survived doing what he did. So anyway, he made his contact, and yes, *mea culpa*, *mea culpa* – I should have known he did that.'

If he'd been hoping Diana Taverner would wave his guilt away, he was disappointed.

'Anyway.' Moving briskly on. 'Having made contact, he convinces whoever, let's call him Hans, he convinces Hans he's built up a network of people prepared to pass on whatever titbits their professional lives offer. The same kind of thing we'd be interested in ourselves. Now, I know you're going to say, "But they're on our side—"'

Because it was his firmly held principle that when trying to seduce, you bowled the odd full toss.

'For God's sake, John. Who do you think you're talking to?'

For information purposes, everyone was an enemy.

'Sorry. So anyway, Hans takes the bait, and in return for a small amount of money, peanuts, he's acquired a string. But strictly sight unseen, of course, because he can't go round kicking tyres, can he? Not with a stable of spooks. All he can do is give thanks, open a bank account so Dieter can feed the fledglings, and sit back and wait for product.'

'Which is what?'

'That's the beauty of it. Hess would've claimed to have long-term agents in place, the kind that take years of cultivation. So there's not going to be major product. Not right away. Which keeps Hans quiet and doesn't worry Dieter one jot, because by the time his debts fall due, and his agents are expected to be coughing up the prover-bial fairy dust, well, he'll be dead. He knows how ill he is. He's not expecting a miracle recovery.'

Diana Taverner's eyebrows were drawn to a point. Partly she was assessing Bachelor's story; partly his demeanour. He seemed to believe his tale, but then, he was invested in it – either Hess's list was the harmless petty larceny Bachelor was selling, or the old fool had really had been up to something, in which case it had been happening on Bachelor's watch. And while her warnings to him about prison time had been for effect, her other threats had been real. Taverner had a strict policy about mistakes. She was prepared to accept her subordinates made them so long as they were prepared to take the blame. She didn't like finding other people's messes on her desk. From a distance, they might look like her own.

On the other hand, surrendering the list was a point in his favour. He could have pretended he'd never found it, and worked up a legend to explain Hess's secret funds. Along with her policy on mistakes, Taverner had one on cover-ups: provided they came with full deniability, she could live with them.

He'd stopped talking.

She said, 'And all this for a few extra quid.'

'Don't discount it. We don't exactly bed them down in clover—'

'Don't talk to me, John. Talk to the minister. And she can talk to the Treasury.'

'Well, quite. But anyway, a few extra quid, a couple of grand a year, makes the difference to Dieter between a nice bottle of wine and a supermarket offer.' Bachelor paused, having been struck by a vision of his own future. Where was he? Yes: 'And besides . . . He was a game old bird. He probably enjoyed it.'

'Maybe so,' she said.

The moment's silence they shared was more of a wake for Dieter Hess than the evening in the pub had been.

She said, 'Okay. You screwed up, which I'm not forgetting, but for the moment, no harm done. Hans'll no doubt come looking for his strays once he's sure Dieter's safely forgotten, so Hess's phantoms are on your watch list. I don't want to read about various shut-ins being smothered in their sleep when a vengeful BND spook finds he's been conned.'

Bachelor didn't reply. He was staring at a fixed point in space that was either high above London or somewhere in the back of his own mind. Lady Di scowled. If anyone was going to fall prey to reverie in her office, it was her.

'Still with me?'

'There's another possibility.'

'Enlighten me.'

'You're right. Hans, whoever he is, will wait for the ashes to settle before he comes looking for Dieter's lost sheep. Which gives us a window of opportunity.'

Lady Di leaned back. 'Go on.'

'This younger girl, the one Hess must have meant for show . . . What if we turn her?'

'You want to recruit her?'

'Why not? If she's suitable . . . We run the usual background checks, make sure she's not an idiot or a nutjob, but if she fits the asset profile, why not? Hans already thinks she's on his side, and she doesn't even know he exists. We'd have a ready-made double. How much of a coup is that?'

'Running an op against a friendly?'

'It wouldn't be an op as such. If Hans is planning a recruitment drive on our soil, it serves him right if he gets his fingers burnt. Don't pretend you don't like the idea.'

As far as Diana Taverner was concerned, she'd pretend whatever she liked. But she allowed the idea to percolate while she told Bachelor to leave, and he departed to float round Regent's Park, wondering whether he'd done enough to save his career.

Recruit one of Hess's phantoms . . . It had a nice circularity to it. Was the kind of scheme which could become a case study, a model for future strategists to ponder; how to seize an opportunity, turn it into a triumph. Back door views into other states' intelligence services were always welcome. Like having the chance to rummage through your best friend's cupboards. An opportunity you'd publicly deplore, but so long as they didn't find out about it, you were never going to pass up.

And as so often with Second-Desk decisions, it was the money that tilted the balance. When the money side of it occurred to her, a slow smile spread across Diana Taverner's face; a smile that had been known to draw men her way, until they got close enough to notice that it never reached her eyes. Hans had been paying Hess to maintain his network; he'd be disappointed when he discovered nine tenths of this network was fake, but if he thought the girl was genuine, he'd continue paying her upkeep. Which meant the Park wouldn't have to. A detail that would bring her a standing ovation once she ran it past the Limitations Committee.

She had Bachelor paged, and gave him the go-ahead.

The waves were mostly froth: great fat spumes hurling themselves at the Cobb's sides, then spitting as high as they could reach before collapsing back into the roiling puddle of the sea. Again and again the waves did this, as if reminding the Cobb that, while it might have graced this harbour for hundreds of years, the sea had been around significantly longer, and would prevail in the long run.

That particular scenario wasn't troubling Hannah Weiss, however. Mostly, she was enjoying the figure she must cast to anyone watching from the quay. With a red windcheater and jeans in place of a black cloak, and her dark-blonde hair pulled into the briefest of knots at the back of her head, she was a far cry from Meryl Streep, but still: there was no denying the inherent romance in the scene. The waves splashed against the stone, and the grey sky was tinged with purple on the horizon, threatening rain later, and here she was; lingering on the stone arm Lyme extends into the sea, curled protectively round its bobbing fleet of boats.

And she was here with romantic purpose, of course. The man who had dropped into her life a mere fortnight earlier had brought her here, or perhaps summoned her was a better way of putting it; or perhaps – to be blunt – had sent her the rail ticket: first class return (big spender!), a cottage for the weekend, and he'd join her, within an hour of her arrival, on the Cobb. Sorry they couldn't travel together, but he'd explain all soonest. Clive Tremain, he was called. He wore a tie all week and polos all weekend, enjoyed country walks and well-earned pub meals after, and was going to do his damnedest to borrow a dog for this particular mini-break, so they could throw balls on a beach, and watch it jump across waves to collect them.

He'd turned up at a party two weeks earlier, an old friend of an old friend of the party-giver, and had cornered Hannah in the kitchen for an hour, hung avidly on her every word, then wooed her number out of her before mysteriously disappearing. She'd been on tenterhooks for forty-eight hours, which was her upper limit for tenterhooks, before he'd used it. Since then they'd been on three dates and he'd improved on each occasion, though had yet to make any significant moves in a bedward direction. And then came the weekend-in-Lyme-Regis idea, which struck Hannah as perfect, definitely one up on any invitation any of her girlfriends had yet received. Clive Tremain. A bit sticky-looking at first sight – sticky-looking as in, might just have a stick stuck up him – but that didn't detract from his looks. He had the air of one who'd taken orders in the past, and might not be above dishing them out in the future.

And now here he came, for this surely must be him – a man approaching the Cobb from the road. Wearing a black overcoat at which la Streep herself might not have turned her nose up, and bareheaded, and on the Cobb itself now, near enough for a pang of disappointment to reach her, because it wasn't Clive; was a much older man . . . She turned, glad she hadn't embarrassed herself with a wave, and keen to resume her solitary vigil over the sea, striking just the right attitude for the real Clive to admire, once he arrived, which he surely would do any minute.

'Ms Weiss?'

She turned.

'Hannah, yes?'

And that was all it took for her to know that Clive Tremain wasn't coming to collect her; that Clive Tremain wasn't showing up in her life ever again. That Clive Tremain, in fact, had never existed at all.

Hannah Weiss. Born '91, parents Joe and Esme – such a lovely name John Bachelor had to say it again, for the sheer pleasure of the sound: *Esme* – *née* Klein, the rest of whose family were scattered across Germany like so many seedlings: Munich mostly, but enough of a contingent in Berlin for there always to be a cousinly bunk for Hannah to bed down in when, as so often during the noughties, she had spent summer vacations there; enjoying the feeling of being truly European, with a language under her belt, and friendly faces to speak it to. Then a degree at Exeter, a proper one: history. And then the Civil Service exam, and now a first-rung job at BIS, which John Bachelor made a bit of a production out of not being sure what it stood for: something to do with business, I'm guessing, Hannah, yes? Something clever to do with business? He was a different man today, John Bachelor, having donned handler's garb, which for Hannah he had decided meant Favourite Uncle.

'Business, Innovation and Skills.'

'The department for,' he said. 'Well done. Very well done.'

They were in a pub off Lyme's main street, the one that curled uphill in picturesque fashion, and Bachelor had already laid a world of apology at

Hannah's feet for what was obviously unforgivable – what couldn't possibly be countenanced for any reason other than the one he was about to produce – and had commenced wooing her with the best the pub had to offer, which was a not-bad prawn risotto and a decent Chablis. The rocky part, he hoped – if only the first of many rocky parts – was over, because she had after all listened to him when he'd explained that Clive wasn't going to be able to make it actually, but that he himself would very much like a quiet word.

Laying that snare for her – the word was honeytrap – was risky, but Bachelor had deemed it necessary; partly to remove her from her usual sphere, because recruitment was best done in a neutral zone, one in which the object of desire had nobody, nothing, to rely on but her own judgement. But it was partly, too – though this could never be spoken – to establish a certain willingness in advance: the object of affection was here to be wooed, true, but the end result was already flagged up. The atmosphere had prepped a 'yes'. The food was warm; the wine was chilled.

Outside, rain danced brightly on the road and pavements and the roofs of parked cars, for the weather Hannah had watched approaching from the Cobb had arrived to complete the scene.

He would like to buy her lunch, he had explained, to make up for Clive's absence. And afterwards, she could head back to London – first class – or, if she preferred, make use of the cottage Clive had booked. Bachelor himself, he hastily added, would not be included.

'There's something going on, isn't there?'

He could scarcely deny this.

'You're not planning on drugging me for sex or anything, are you? You don't look the type, I must say.'

He was grateful for this, until she added: 'Too wrecked looking, really.' She'd looked back towards the sea then, and the purple-fringed cloud in the decreasing distance. 'I take self-defence classes, by the way.'

'Very wise,' said Bachelor, who knew she didn't.

'Okay.' This had been abrupt. 'If that sod's not coming, you'll have to do. Buy me lunch.'

Over which he asked her about herself and her family, and checked her answers against what he already knew, which was almost everything.

'And why did you stop going to Germany, actually, Hannah? Fall out with the cousins?'

'Well, I haven't stopped going,' she said. 'I just haven't been in a while, that's all. I was in the States one year . . .'

Coast to coast, Bachelor mentally supplied; a six-week road-trip with three friends from uni. Hannah had split with her half of the male couple within days of arriving home.

'. . . and just been *really busy* since, but I'll certainly be going back next time I get a sniff of a chance at a decent break. They work you awfully hard, you know.'

'Oh, I'm sure it'll get easier after a while.'

Later, when the rain had passed over, and the sun was making a valiant attempt to regain control, they took a footpath leading out of town, and Bachelor explained a little more of the circumstances that had brought him to her.

'So you mean . . . What, this man stole my identity?'

'In a manner of speaking.'

'But he wasn't racking up huge debts or anything?'

'No, nothing like that. He was using your name and your background, that's all, to convince some people that he had recruited you as what we like to call an asset.'

'A spy.'

'Not really. Well, sort of,' Bachelor amended, when he noticed a certain shine in her eyes.

'So that's what you are too. You're a spy.'

'Yes.'

'And Clive too.'

'Clive's not really his name.'

'Will I see him again?'

'I see no reason why not,' John Bachelor lied.

But there was something in her attitude that hinted that Clive, anyway, had already been written out of her future.

'So what do I do about it?' she asked. 'Do I have to give evidence in court? Something like that?'

'Good heavens, no. Besides, he's dead now.'

She nodded wisely.

'Lord, don't think that. He had a bad heart. He was unwell for a long time. It was only afterwards that we – I – found out what he'd been up to.'

'So nobody knew.'

'That's right.'

'And nobody would still know – I mean, I wouldn't – if you hadn't just told me.'

'That's right.'

In the very best of cases, the object of affection wooed herself.

'So that means you want me to do something for you, doesn't it? I mean, you're hardly telling me all this just to keep me informed. Spies keep secrets. They don't go round blabbing them to all and sundry.'

'They're certainly not supposed to,' he said, thinking of J. K. Coe.

They were under trees, and a sudden gust of wind shook loose some hoarded rain, sprinkling their heads. This made Hannah laugh, and Bachelor had a sudden pang – when she did this, she seemed about thirteen, which was far too young to be wooed or honeytrapped; far too young to be recruited. But when her laughter stopped, the look she directed at him was old enough that he shook those thoughts away.

'You want me to make it real, don't you? To become what he pretended I was. Except you want me to do this while really being on your side.'

'It's not something anyone's going to ask you to do,' he said. 'It's simply an idea that's been . . . floated.'

As if the idea had risen out of nowhere, and was bobbing even now between them like a balloon, red as the coat she wore. She could burst it with a word. If she did, he would do nothing to attempt to change her mind. Nothing at all. He swore this to himself on everything he kept holy, if anything still bore that description. And even if his failure to recruit her swept him straight back into Lady Di's black books, he'd deal with that – even unto being cast out of Regent's Park, into the pit of unemployability that awaited a man his age, with what was effectively a blank CV –

sooner than strong-arm this young woman into leading a shadow life.

Because that's what he'd been leading, these decades gone. A shadow life. Scurrying round the fringes of other people's history, ensuring that none of it ever raised its head in polite company.

She was looking up into the trees, awaiting the next shower.

John Bachelor knew enough not to say anything.

He watched her though, and marvelled again at what it must be like to be young, and know that you hadn't yet messed everything up. In Hannah's case, he thought, she'd continue looking young well into age. Bone structure counted. He might be trying to steal her soul, just as dead Dieter Hess had stolen her identity, but ultimately Hannah Weiss would hang on to everything that made her who she really was. That, too, he marvelled at, a trick he'd not managed himself.

She said, 'Will it be dangerous?'

'Not like in the films.'

'You don't know what kind of films I watch.

I don't mean car chases and jumping out of helicopters. I mean going to prison. Being caught and locked up. That kind of dangerous.'

'Sometimes,' Bachelor said. 'That happens sometimes. Not very often.'

'And will I get training?'

'Yes. But it'll all have to be done in secret. As far as anyone knows, you'll still be the girl you always were. Woman, I mean.'

'Yes. You mean woman.'

She looked upwards again, as if the answer to her questions sat hidden among leaves. And then she looked at John Bachelor.

'Okay,' she said.

'Okay?'

'I'll do it. I'll be your spy.'

'Good,' he said, and then, as if trying to convince himself, he said it again. 'Good.'

It was three months later that Jackson Lamb made an unaccustomed field trip. Hertfordshire was his destination: he'd received advance word of a wholesale spirits outlet going down the tubes, and had hopes of picking up a case or two of Scotch at knockdown prices.

It was a long journey to make on the off-chance, so he went on a work day, and made River Cartwright drive.

'This is official business?'

'It's the Secret Service, Cartwright. Not everything we do is officially sanctioned.'

Two hours later, with a satisfied Lamb in the back seat, and two cases of Famous Grouse in the boot, they were heading back towards the capital.

Three hours later, with a rather more disgruntled Lamb in the back seat, they were still heading back towards the capital.

'This is supposed to be a short cut?'

'I never claimed it was a short cut,' River said. 'I explained it was a diversion. A lorry shed its load on the — were you actually listening?'

'Blah blah motorway, blah blah road closure,' Lamb said. 'If I'd known it was a magical mystery tour, I might have paid attention. Where are we?'

'Just coming out of St Albans. And you're not smoking that.'

Lamb sighed. In return for River driving him, buying lunch and not having the damn radio on, Lamb had agreed not to smoke in the car, and was starting to wonder how he'd let himself be bested. 'Turn in here,' he said.

'A cemetery?'

'Does it have a No Smoking sign?'

River parked just beyond the stone gateway.

Lamb got out of the car and lit a cigarette. The cemetery was basic, a recent development; had no Gothic-looking statuary, and was essentially a lawn with dividing hedges and headstones. A wide path led to the far end, which was awaiting occupants, and here and there were standpipes where visitors could fill watering cans, with which to tend the plots of their beloveds. Lamb, who carried his dead round with him, didn't spend a lot of time in graveyards. This one didn't seem busy, but perhaps Wednesday afternoons were a slack period.

St Albans was ringing a bell, though. He sorted through his mental files, and came up with the name Dieter Hess. Who'd run a ghost network from here, and had now joined one of his own.

Wondering if Hess was nearby, and to give himself time to smoke more, Lamb wandered up the path. The only other human in sight was an elderly woman sitting on a bench, possibly planning ahead. At the far end he counted down a row of newer headstones. Sure enough, third along was Dieter Hess's; a simple stone with just his name and dates. A lot of story crammed between two numbers.

Lamb regarded the stone. A ghost network. The lengths some people go to for a few extra quid, he thought; but knew, too, that the money hadn't been all of it. The reason they called it The Game was that there were always those ready to play, even if that meant switching sides. Ideology, too, was just another excuse.

But now the old boy was buried, and no harm done. At least, Lamb hoped there was no harm done . . . He didn't trust dying messages, and Hess's posthumous list fell under that heading. When something was hidden, but not so well that it couldn't be found, the possibility existed that that had been the intention. And if a ghost network consisted of nine shut-ins and one living breathing young woman, well: a suspicious mind might think that resembled bait.

He dropped his cigarette and ground it under-foot. It was too much of a stretch, he conceded. Would have meant that the hypothetical Hans, far from being Dieter Hess's dupe, was truly cunning: paying Hess simply to hide a coded list under his carpet, knowing that when he pegged out, his flat would be steam-cleaned – when a spy passes, his cupboards need clearing out. So the tenth name would come into the hands of the Service, and maybe – just maybe – its owner, already in the employ of the BND, would be adopted by MI5.

And what looked like a ready-made double would become, in fact, a triple.

But plots need willing players. Lamb could accept that a young woman with a sense of adven-ture might let herself be recruited by a foreign service in her teens, but didn't think John Bachelor had the nous to play his part, and re-recruit her in turn; or, come to that, that Diana Taverner would give him the green light to do so. Taverner was ambitious, but she wasn't stupid. Too bad for Hans, then. Sometimes you put a lot of effort into schemes that never paid off. Everyone had days like that, though today – thinking of the booty in the boot – wasn't one of Lamb's.

An atavistic impulse had him bend over, find a pebble, and place it on Hess's headstone.

One old spook to another, he thought, then headed back to the car.

Later that same afternoon, Hannah Weiss made her way home by Tube. It had been a good day. Her probation at BIS was over; her supervisor had given her two thumbs up, and let her know that great things were expected of her. This could mean anything, of course; that a lifetime of key performance indicators and quarterly assessments lay ahead; or that her career would stretch down Whitehall's corridors, far into an unimaginable distance. 'Great things' could mean Cabinet level. It wasn't impossible. She had influential support, after all, even if it had to remain covert. This was the life she had chosen.

She changed at Piccadilly, and found herself standing on a platform next to a middle-aged man in a white raincoat. He carried a rolled-up copy of *Private Eye*. When the train arrived they stepped on board together, and were crammed into a corner of the carriage. The train pulled away, and she found herself leaning against his arm.

For upwards of a minute, the train rattled and lurched through the darkness. And then, just as it began to slow, and the next station hauled into sight, she felt him shift so that his lips were above her ear.

'*Wir sind alle sehr stolz auf dich*, Hannah,' he said. Then the train halted, the doors opened, and he was gone.

We're all very proud of you.

A fresh crowd enveloped Hannah Weiss. Deep inside its beating heart, she hugged secret knowledge to herself.

THE DROP

S EASONED PARK WATCHERS later said that the affair really began in Fischer's, that beloved 'café and konditorei' that bestows a touch of early twentieth-century Vienna on the foothills of twenty-first-century Marylebone High Street; its warm interior, its spring yellows and glazed browns, a welcome refuge from the winter-drizzled pavements. The more callow of their brethren preferred to believe that it started, as all things must, at Regent's Park itself, but then the new generation had been trained to think itself at the constant heart of events, while the older knew that Spook Street, like Watling Street, runs backwards and forwards in time. The meeting at the Park might well have occurred earlier than the drop on Marylebone High, but that was a detail only, and when the time came for the whole business to be black-ribboned and consigned to the archive, nobody would care that a strip-lit office with functional furniture had been where the starting pistol was fired. No, once the facts were safely recorded, they'd print the legend instead. And legends thrive on local colour.

So Fischer's was the starting point; as good a place as any, and better than most. To quote from its website, 'The menu includes an extensive choice of cured fish, salads, schnitzels, sausages, *brötchen* and sandwiches, *strudels*, biscuits, ice-cream coupes, hot chocolates and coffees with traditional *tortes mit schlag*.' How could that not set the heart racing, with its enticing umlauts, its brazen italics, its artfully roman 'coupes'? Solomon Dortmund can never pick up its menu without feeling that life – even one as long as his – holds some con-solations; can never put it down again without inner turmoil having raged.

Today, he has settled upon a hot chocolate – he

breakfasted late, so has no need for anything substantial, but various errands having placed him in the neighbourhood, it would be unthinkable to pass Fischer's without dropping in. And his appearance is instantly celebrated: he is greeted by name by a friendly young waiter, he is guided to a table, he is assured that his chocolate has so nearly arrived that he might as well be dabbing a napkin to his lips already. To all of which Solomon, being one of those heroes whom life's cruelties have rendered gentle, responds with a kind smile. Secure at his table, he surveys the congregation: sparse today, but other people, however few in number, always command Solomon's interest, for Solomon is a people-watcher: always has been, always will be. His life having included many people who disappeared too soon, he is attentive to those who remain within sight, which today include an elderly pair sitting beneath the clock, and whose conversation, he feels, will mirror that device's progress, being equally regular, equally familiar, equally unlikely to surprise; three intense young men, heavily bearded, discussing politics (he hopes), or at least literature, or chess; and a pair of women in their forties who are absorbed in something one of them has summoned up on her telephone. Solomon nods benevolently. His own telephone is black, with a rotary dial, and lives on a table, but he is one of those rare creatures who recognises that even those technological developments in which he himself has neither interest nor investment might yet be of value to others, and he is perfectly content to allow them to indulge themselves. Such contemplation happily consumes the time needed to prepare his chocolate, for here comes the waiter already, and soon all is neatly arranged in front of him: cup, saucer, spoon, napkin; the elements of ritual as important as the beverage itself. Solomon Dortmund, eyes closed, takes a sip, and for one tiny moment is transported to his childhood. Few who knew him then would recognise him now. That robust child, the roly-poly infant, is now stooped and out of synch with the world. In his black coat and antique homburg, whiskers sprouting from every visible orifice, he resembles an academic whose subject has been rendered otiose. A figure of fun to those who don't know him, and he is aware of that, and regards it as one of life's better jokes. He takes another sip. This is not heaven; this is not perfection. But it is a small moment of pleasure in a world more commonly disposed to pain, and is to be treasured.

Sated for the moment, he resumes his inspection of the room. To his left, by the window, is a young blonde woman, and Solomon allows his gaze to linger on her, for this young woman is very attractive, in today's idiom; *beautiful* in Solomon's own, for Solomon is too old to pay heed to the ebb and flow of linguistic fashion, and he knows beauty when he sees it. The young woman is sorting through correspondence, which gives Solomon a little flush of pleasure, for who today, young or old, sorts through correspondence? Ninety per cent of what drops through his own letterbox is junk; the other ten per cent mere notifications of one sort or another: meter readings, interest rates; nothing requiring a response. But this young lady has a number of envelopes in front of her; brown envelopes of the size codified as C5 (Solomon Dortmund knows his stationery). Job applications? He dabs his lips with his napkin. He enjoys these little excursions into the lives of others, the raising of unanswerable questions. He has solved, or reconciled himself to, all the puzzles his own life is likely to throw at him. Other people's remain a source of fascination. Glimpses of their occupations are overheard prayers; doors left ajar on mysterious existences.

He returns to his chocolate, slowing down his intake, because endings should never be hurried. Once more, he surveys the room. The young woman has gathered her things together; is standing, preparing to leave. A man enters, his attention on his mobile phone. Through the momentarily open door intrude the mid-morning sounds of Marylebone High: a passing taxi, a skirl of laughter, the rumble of London. And Solomon can see what is about to happen as surely as if he were reading the scene on a page; the brief moment of impact, the startled *oomph* from the young lady, an equally surprised *ungh* from the man, a scattering of envelopes, the sudden monopoly of attention. It takes less time to happen than it does to recount. And then the man, fully recovered, is apologising; the young woman assuring him that the fault is as much hers as his (this is not true); the envelopes are gathered up while the young lady pats at herself, confirming that she still has everything she ought to have; the bag slung over her shoulder, the scarf around her neck. It is done. The stack of envelopes is returned to her with a smile, a nod; there would have been a doffing of a hat, had the props department supplied a hat. A moment later, the man is at a table, busying himself with the buttons on his coat; the young woman is at the door, is through it, is gone. Marylebone High Street has swallowed her up. The morning continues in its unhurried way.

And Solomon Dortmund finishes his chocolate, and at length rises and settles his bill, a scrupulous ten per cent added in coins. To anyone watching as he heads for the outside world, he is no more than old-fashioned clothing on a stick-like frame; a judgement he would accept without demur. But under the hat, under the coat, under the wealth of whiskers, Solomon carries the memory of tradecraft in his bones, and those bones are rattled now by more than the winter wind.

'John,' he says to himself as he steps onto the pavement. 'I must speak to John.'

And then he too dissolves into London's mass.

Meanwhile – or sometime earlier, by the pedant's clock; the previous week, or the one before that – there was a meeting in Regent's Park. A strip-lit office, as mentioned, with functional furniture and carpet tiles, each replaceable square foot a forgettable colour and texture. The table commanding most of the floor space had two saucer-sized holes carved into it, through which cables could be threaded when hardware needed plugging in, and along one wall was a whiteboard which, to Diana Taverner's certain knowledge, had never been used, but which nevertheless mutely declared itself the room's focal point. The chairs were H&S-approved, but only to the extent that each could hold an adult's weight; long-term occupation of any would result in backache. So far, so good, she thought. The head of the Limitations Committee was expected, and Lady Di liked to lean austeritywards on such occasions, Oliver Nash having made something of a circus, on his last visit, of harrumphing at whatever he deemed unnecessary extravagance. His singling out of a print on her wall, a perfectly modest John Piper, still rankled. Today, then, the only hint of luxury was the plate of pastries neatly placed between the table's two utility holes. Raisin-studded, chocolate-sprinkled, icing-sugar-frosted, the patisserie might have been assembled for a weekend supplement photo shoot. A pile of napkins sat next to them. On a smaller table in the corner was a pot of filter coffee and a stack of takeaway cups. It had taken her ten minutes to get it all just right.

She had rinsed her hands in the nearby bathroom; stuffed the box the pastries came in into the nearest cupboard. By the time she heard the lift arrive, by the time the door opened, she was in one of the dreadful chairs; a notebook in front of her, a pen, still capped, lying in the ridge between its open pages.

'Diana. Ravishing as always.'

'Oliver. Have you lost weight?'

It was an open secret that Nash had been attempting one diet or another for some time; long enough, indeed, for the cruel suggestion to be made that if he'd attempted them sequentially instead of all at once, one of them might have proved effective.

The look he gave her was not entirely free of suspicion. 'I might have,' he said.

'Oh, I'm positive. But please, sit. Sit. I've poured you a coffee.'

He did so. 'Rather spartan accommodation.'

'Needs must, Oliver. We save the larger rooms for group sessions. Less wear and tear, and saves on heating, of course. I must apologise for this, by the way.' She gestured at, without looking towards, the plate of pastries. 'They're for the departmental gathering, I can't think why they've been brought in here. Somebody got their wires crossed.'

'*Hmph*. Stretching the budget a little, wouldn't you say?'

'Oh, out of my own pocket. A little treat for the boys and girls on the hub. They work so hard.'

'We're all very grateful.'

His sandy hair had thinned in the last months, as if in mockery of his attempts to lose weight elsewhere, but his chins remained prominent. Fastidiously avoiding looking at the plate of pastries, he placed his hands on his paunch, and fixed his gaze on Diana. 'How's the ship? Come through choppy seas lately, haven't we?'

'If we'd wanted a quiet life, we'd have joined the fire brigade.'

'Well, so long as we're all having fun.' He seemed to realise that the placement of his hands emphasised the roundness of his stomach and shifted them to the tabletop, a more dynamic posture. 'So. Snow White.' He raised an eyebrow. 'By the way, have I mentioned—'

'Everybody's mentioned.'

'— what a ridiculous codename that is?'

'They're randomly assigned.'

'I mean, what if it had been Goldilocks, for God's sake?'

'We might have had to re-roll the dice. But as things stand, we live with it.'

'Do you ever feel that we've become slaves to the processes? Rather than their existing to facilitate our objectives?'

He had always been one for the arch observation, even when the observation in question was of unadorned banality.

'Let's save that for Wants and Needs, shall we?' she said, meaning the bi-monthly interdepartmental catch-up most people termed Whines and Niggles. 'Snow White. You've received the request. There's no difficulty, surely?'

But Oliver Nash preferred being in the driving seat, and would take whatever damn route he chose.

'If memory serves,' he said, 'and it usually does, she was recruited by an older chap.'

'John Bachelor.'

'But here she is being handled by a new boy. How'd that come about?'

'It was felt that Bachelor wasn't up to the job.'

'Why?'

'Because he wasn't up to the job.'

'Ah. Got on your wrong side, did he?'

'I have no wrong sides, Oliver. I just find the occasional thorn in one, that's all.'

Not that he had been particularly thorny, John Bachelor, since that would have required more character than he possessed. He was, rather, an also-ran; constantly sidelined throughout his career; ultimately parked on the milk round, the name given to the aftercare service provided to pensioned-off assets. Bachelor's remit – which, in the last round of cuts, had been downgraded to 'irregular' – involved ensuring that his charges remained secure, that no passes had been made in their direction; increasingly, that they were still alive and in possession of their marbles. They were Cold War foot soldiers, for the most part, who had risked their younger lives pilfering secrets for the West, and were eking out what time remained to them on Service pensions. A dying breed, in every sense.

But they had careers, or at least activities, to look back on with pride. John Bachelor, on the other hand, had little more than a scrapbook full of service station receipts and the memory of a lone triumph: the recruitment of Snow White.

'And this new chap – Pynne? Richard Pynne?'

'He's not that new.'

'Bet that name gave him sleepless nights as a boy.'

'Luckily the Service isn't your old prep school. He'll be along in a moment. And – forgive me, I can't resist. I had to skip breakfast.'

She helped herself to an almond croissant, took a dainty nibble from one end, and placed it carefully on a napkin.

'An extra five minutes on the treadmill,' she said.

There was a knock on the door, and Richard Pynne appeared.

'You two haven't met,' Taverner said. 'Oliver Nash, chair of Limitations, and one of the great and the good, as you won't need me to tell you, Richard. Oliver, this is Richard Pynne. Richard was Cambridge, I'm afraid, but you'll just have to forgive him.'

'No great rivalry between Cambridge and the LSE, Diana, as I'm sure you remember all too well.' Without getting up, he extended a hand, and Pynne shook it.

'A pleasure, sir.'

'Help yourself to a pastry, Richard. Oliver was about to ask for a rundown on Snow White's request.'

'Do you want me to . . .'

'In your own time.'

Pynne sat. He was a large young man, and had dealt with a rapidly receding hairline by shaving his head from his teenage years; this, combined with thick-framed spectacles, lent him a geeky look which wasn't aided by his somewhat hesitant manner of speech. But he had a fully working brain, had scored highly on the agent-running scenarios put together across the river, and Snow White was a home-soil operation: low risk. Di Taverner didn't play favourites. She'd been known, though, to back winners. If Pynne handled his first joe without mishap he might find himself elevated above shift manager on the hub, his current role.

'Snow White's been having problems at BIS,' he began.

'The Department for Business, Innovation and Skills,' proclaimed Nash. 'And I'd have a lot more confidence in its ability to handle all or any of those things if it could decide whether or not it was using a comma. What kind of problems?'

'Personnel.'

'Personal?'

'Onn*el*,' stressed Pynne. 'Though it covers both, I suppose.'

Nash looked at the pastries and sighed. 'We'd better start at the beginning.'

In the beginning, Snow White – Hannah Weiss – was a civil servant, a fast-track graduate; indistinguishable from any other promising young thing hacking out a career in Whitehall's jungle, except that she'd been recruited at a young age by the BND – the Bundesnachrichtendienst, the German intelligence service. It was always useful to have agents in place, even when the spied-upon was nominally an ally. Especially when fault lines were appearing the length and breadth of Europe. So far so what, as one of Pynne's generation might have ventured; this kind of low-level game-playing was part of the territory, and rarely resulted in more than the odd black eye, a bloodied nose. But this game was different. Hannah's 'recruitment', it transpired, had been carried out without her awareness or consent: she had been no more than a name on a list fraudulently compiled by one Dieter Hess, himself a superannuated asset, one of the pensioners on John Bachelor's milk round. Hess, a shakedown of his cupboards had revealed after his death, had been supplementing his income by running a phantom network, his list consisting of shut-ins and lockaways, for each of whom the BND had been shelling out a small but regular income. Hannah Weiss alone had been living flesh, and unaware of her role in Hess's scheme. She was the one warm body in a league of ghosts.

It was John Bachelor who had uncovered Hess's

deception, and Bachelor who'd come up with the idea of recruiting Hannah, then about to embark on her career in the Civil Service, and allowing the BND to continue thinking her its creature. It had been a bright idea, even Taverner allowed; the one creative spark of Bachelor's dimly lit career, but even then, the flint had been pure desperation. In the absence of his injury-time coup, Bachelor's neck would have been on the block. As it was, he'd scraped up enough credibility to hang on to his job, and Hannah Weiss, whom the BND thought in its employ, had been recruited by the Service, which, in return for low-grade Whitehall gossip, was building up a picture of how the BND ran its agents in the field.

Because it was always useful to have agents in place, even when the spied-upon was nominally an ally . . .

'Snow White's been doing well at BIS, but she feels, and I agree, that it's time for her to move on. There are offices where she'd be more valuable to the BND, which would mean, in return, that we get a peek at their more high-level practices.

The more value they place on her, the more resources they'll expend.'

'Yes, we get the basic picture,' said Nash. He shot a look at Diana, who was taking another bite from her croissant, and seemed, in that moment, to be utterly transported. 'But I thought we didn't want to get too ambitious. Maintain a solid career profile. We turn her into a shooting star, and put her in Number 10 or whatever, the BND'll smell a rat.'

'Yes. But there've been, like I say, personnel problems, and this gives us an iron-clad reason for a switch.'

'Tell.'

'Snow White's manager has developed something of a crush on her.'

'Oh, God.'

'Late night phone calls, unwanted gifts, constant demands for one-on-one meetings that turn inappropriate. It's an unhappy situation.'

'I can imagine. But this manager, can't he be—'

'She.'

'Ah. Well, regardless, can't she be dealt with in-house? It's hardly unprecedented.'

Diana Taverner said, 'She could be. But, as Richard says, it provides us with an opportunity for a shuffling exercise. And we're not suggesting Snow White be moved to Number 10. There is, though, one particular minister whose office is expanding rapidly.'

'The Brexit Secretary, I suppose.'

'Precisely. A move there would be perfectly logical, given Snow White's background. German speakers are at a premium, I'd have thought.'

Oliver Nash pressed a finger to his chin. 'The Civil Service don't like it when we stir their pot.'

'But there's a reason they're called servants.'

'Not the most diplomatic of arguments.' He looked at Pynne. 'This suggestion came from Snow White herself?'

'She's keen to move. It's that or make an official complaint.'

'Which would be a black mark against her,' Diana said.

'Surely not,' said Nash, with heavy sarcasm. His gaze shifted from one to the other, but snagged on the plate of pastries. It was to this he finally spoke: 'Well, I suppose it'll all look part of the general churn. Tell her to make a formal transfer application. It'll be approved.'

'Thank you, sir.'

'Do take one of these, Richard. They're best fresh.'

Richard Pynne thanked her too, took a raisin pastry, and left the room.

'There,' said Lady Di. 'Nice to get something done without umpteen follow-up meetings.' She made a note in her book, then closed it. 'So good of you to make the time.'

'I hope young Pynne isn't taking a gamble with our Snow White just to cheer his CV up. Making himself look good is one thing. But if he blows her usefulness in the process, that'll be down to you.'

'It's all down to me, Oliver. Always is. You know that.'

'Yes, well. Sometimes it's better to stick than twist. There are dissenting voices, you know. An op like this, misinforming a friendly Service, well, I know it comes under the heading fun and games, but it still costs. And that's without considering the blowback if the wheels come off. We rely on the BND's cooperation with counterterrorism. All pulling together. What'll it look like if they find we've been yanking their chain?'

'They keep secrets, we keep secrets. That, as you put it, is where the fun and games comes in. And let's not forget the only reason we have Snow White is that the BND thought they were running a network on our soil. What's sauce for the goose goes well with the schnitzel, don't you think? More coffee?'

'I shouldn't.'

But he pushed his cup towards her anyway.

Lady Di took it, crossed to the table in the corner, and poured him another cup. When she turned, he was reaching for a pastry.

She made sure not to be smiling on her return.

Solomon Dortmund said: 'It was a drop.'

'Well, I'm sure something was dropped—'

'It was a *drop*.'

When he was excited, Solomon's Teutonic roots

showed. This was partly, John Bachelor thought, a matter of his accent hardening; partly a whole body shift, as if the ancient figure, balancing a bone china teacup on a bone china saucer and not looking much more robust than either, had developed a sudden steeliness within. He was, like most of those in Bachelor's care, an ambassador from another era, one in which hardship was familiar to young and old alike, and in which certainty was not relinquished lightly. Solomon knew what he knew. He knew he had seen a drop.

'She was a young thing, twenty-two, twenty-three.'

John Bachelor mentally added ten years.

'Blonde and very pretty.'

Of course, because all young women were very pretty. Even the plain were pretty to the old, their youth a dazzling distraction.

'And he was a spook, John.'

'You recognised him?'

'The type.'

'But not the actual person.'

'I'm telling you, I know what I saw.'

He had seen a drop.

Bachelor sighed, without making much attempt to hide it. He had much to sigh about. An icy wind was chasing up and down the nearby Edgware Road, where frost patterned the pavements. His left shoe was letting in damp, and before long would be letting in everything else: the cold, the rain, the inevitable snow. His overcoat was thinner than the weather required; it was ten fifteen, and already he wanted a drink. Not needed, he noted gratefully, but wanted. He did not have the shakes, and he was not hungover. But he wanted a drink.

'Solly,' he said. 'This was Fischer's, on a Tuesday morning. It's a popular place, with a lot of traffic. Don't you think it possible that what you thought you saw was just some accidental interaction?'

'I don't think I saw anything,' the old man said.

Result.

But Bachelor's hopes were no sooner formed than destroyed:

'I *know*. She passed him an envelope. She dropped

a pile, he scooped them up. But one went into his coat pocket.'

'A manila envelope.'

'A manila envelope, yes. This is an important detail? Because you say it—'

'I'm just trying to establish the facts.'

'— you say it as if it were an outlandish item for anyone to be in possession of, on a Tuesday morning. A manila envelope, yes. C5 size. You are familiar with the dimensions?'

Solomon held his hands just so.

'I'm familiar with the dimensions, yes.'

'Good. It was a drop, John.'

In trade terms, a passing on of information, instructions, *product*, in such a manner as to make it seem that nothing had occurred.

Bachelor had things to do; he had an agenda. Top of which was sorting his life out. Next was ensuring he had somewhere to sleep that night. It was likely that the first item would be held over indefinitely, but it was imperative that the second receive his full and immediate attention. And yet, if the milk round had taught John

Bachelor anything, it was that when an old asset got his teeth into something, he wasn't going to let go until a dental mould had been cast.

'Okay,' he said. 'Okay. Have you a sheet of paper I can use? And a pen?'

'They don't supply you with these things?'

Bachelor had no idea whether they did or not. 'They give us pens, but they're actually blowpipes. They're rubbish for writing with.'

Solomon chuckled, because he was getting what he wanted, and rummaged in a drawer for a small notebook and a biro. 'You can keep these,' he said. 'That way you will have a full record of your investigation.'

I'm not an investigator, I'm a nursemaid. But they were past that point. 'Young, blonde, very pretty.' He wrote those words down. On the page, they looked strangely unconvincing. 'Anything else?'

Solomon considered. 'She was nicely dressed.'

Nicely dressed went on a new line.

'And she was drinking tea.'

After a brief internal struggle, Bachelor added this to his list.

Solomon shrugged. 'By the time I knew to pay attention, she was already out of the door.'

'What about the man?'

'He was about fifty, I would say, with brown hair greying at the temples. Clean shaven. No spectacles. He wore a camel-hair coat over a dark suit, red tie. Patterned, with stripes. Black brogues, yellow socks. I noticed them particularly, John. A man who wears yellow socks is capable of anything.'

'I've often thought so,' Bachelor said, but only because Solomon was clearly awaiting a response.

'He ordered coffee and a slice of torte. He was right-handed, John. He held the fork in his right hand.'

'Right-handed,' Bachelor said, making the appropriate note in his book. The clock on the kitchen wall was making long-suffering progress towards twenty past the hour: with a bit of luck, he thought, he'd have grown old and died and be in his coffin by the time the half-hour struck.

'And he was reading the *Wall Street Journal*.'

'He brought that with him?'

'No, he found it on a nearby seat.'

'The one the girl had been using?'

'No.'

'You're sure about that? Think carefully. It could be a crucial detail.'

'I think you are playing the satirist now, John.'

'Maybe a bit.' He looked the older man in the eye. 'Things like this don't happen any more. Drops in cafés? Once upon a time, sure, but nowadays? It's the twenty-first century.' He'd nearly said the twentieth. 'People don't do drops, they don't carry sword-sticks.'

'You think, instead, they deliver information by drone, or just text it to each other?' Solomon Dortmund shook his elderly head. 'Or send it by email perhaps, so some teenager in Korea can post it on Twitter? No, John. There's a reason why people say the old ways are the best. It's because the old ways are the best.'

'You're enjoying this, aren't you?'

'Enjoy? No. I am doing my duty, that is all.'

'And what do you want me to do about it?'

Solomon shrugged. 'Do, don't do, that is up to

you. I was an asset, yes? That is the term you use. Well, maybe I'm not so useful any more, but I know what I saw and I've told you what I know. In the old days, that was enough. I pass the information on.' He actually made a passing motion here, as if handing an invisible baby back to its mother. 'What happens to it afterwards, that was never my concern.'

Bachelor said, 'Well, thanks for the notebook. It will come in handy.'

'You haven't asked me if there is anything else.'

'I'm sorry, Solomon. Was there anything else?'

'Yes. The man's name is Peter Kahlmann.'

'. . . Ah.'

'Perhaps this information will help you trace him?'

'It can't hurt,' said Bachelor, opening the notebook again.

The previous night had been unsatisfactory, to say the least; had been spent on a sofa not long enough, and not comfortable. His current lodgings were reaching the end of their natural lease, which is to say that after one week in the bed of the flat's owner – a former lover – he had spent two in the sitting room, and now the knell had been sounded. On arriving the previous evening, he had found his battered suitcase packed and ready, and it had only been by dint of special pleading, and reference to past shared happinesses – slight and long ago – that he had engineered one final sleepover, not that sleep had made an appearance. When dawn arrived, reluctantly poking its way past the curtains, Bachelor had greeted it with the spirit a condemned man might his breakfast: at least the wait was over, though there was nothing agreeable about what happened next.

And all that had brought him to this point: none of that was pretty either. Especially not the decision to cash in his pension and allow his former brother-in-law to invest the capital – no risk, no gain, John; have to speculate to accumulate – a move intended to secure his financial future, which had been successful, but only in the sense that there was a certain security in knowing one's financial future was unlikely to waver from its present circumstance.

And he had to give this much to the former brother-in-law: he'd finished the job his sister had started. When the lease on Bachelor's 'studio flat' – yeah, right; put a bucket in the corner of a bedsit, and you could claim it was en suite – had come up for renewal last month, he'd been unable to scrape together the fees the letting company required for the burdensome task of doing sweet fuck all. And that was that. How could he possibly be homeless? He worked for Her Majesty's Government. And just to put the icing on the cupcake, his job involved making sure that one-time foreign assets had a place to lay their head, and a cup of sweet tea waiting when they opened their eyes again. They called it the milk round. It might have been a better career choice being an actual fucking milkman, and that was taking into account that nobody had milk delivered any more. At least he'd have got to keep the apron; something to use as a pillow at night.

He was in a pub having these thoughts, having drunk the large Scotch he hadn't needed but wanted, and now working on a second he hadn't thought he wanted but turned out to need. In front of him was the notebook Solomon had given him, and on a fresh page he was making a list of possible next moves. There were no other ex-lovers to be tapped up, not if he valued his genitals. *Hotel*, he'd already crossed out. His credit cards had been thrashed to within an inch of their lives; they'd combust in the daylight like vampires. *Estate agents* he'd also scored through. The amount of capital you needed to set yourself up in a flat, a bedsit, a vacant stretch of corridor in London, was so far beyond a joke it had reached the other side and become funny again. How did anyone manage this? There was a good reason, he now understood, why unhappy marriages survived, and it was this: an unhappy marriage at least had two people supporting it. Once you cut yourself loose, disinvested from the marital property, you could either look forward to a life way down on the first rung or move to, I don't know, the fucking North.

But let's not get too wrapped up in self-pity, John. Worse comes to worst, you can sleep in your car.

Bachelor sighed and made inroads on his drink. At the top of this downward spiral was work, and the downgrading of his role to 'irregular', which was HR for part-time. A three-day week, with concomitant drop in salary: You won't mind, will you, John? Look on it as a toe in the waters of retirement . . . He'd be better off being one of his own charges. Take Solomon Dortmund. Dortmund was a million years old, sure, and had seen rough times, and it wasn't like Bachelor begrudged him safe harbour, but still: he had that little flat, and a pension to keep him in coffee and cake. There'd been a moment an hour ago when he'd nearly asked Solomon the favour: a place to kip for a night or two. Just until he worked out something permanent. But he was glad he hadn't. Not that he thought the old man would have refused him. But Bachelor couldn't have borne his pity.

Feisty old bugger, though.

'I waited until he'd left,' Solomon had said. 'There is always something to do on the High Street. You know the marvellous bookshop?'

'Everyone does.'

'And then I returned and had a word with the waiter. They all know me there.'

'And they knew your man? By name?'

'He is a regular. Once or twice, he has made a booking. So yes, the waiter knew his name just as he knows mine.'

'And was happy to tell you?'

'I said I thought I recognised him, but too late to say hello. A nephew of an old friend I was anxious to be in touch with.' Solomon had given an odd little smile, half pride, half regret. 'It is not difficult to pretend to be a confused old man. A harmless, confused old man.'

Bachelor had said, 'You're a piece of work, Solly. Okay, I'll raise this back at the Park. See what they can do with the name.'

And now he flicked back a page and looked again: Peter Kahlmann. German-sounding. It meant nothing, and the thought of turning up at Regent's Park and asking for a trace to be run was kind of funny; beyond satire, actually. John Bachelor wasn't welcome round Regent's Park.

Along with the irregular status went a degree of
autonomy; which meant, in essence, that nobody
gave a damn about his work. The milk round
had a built-in obsolescence; five years, give or
take, and his charges would be in their graves.
For now, he made a written report once a month,
unless an emergency happened – death or hospi-
talisation – and kept well clear until summoned.
And this non-status was largely down to the
Hannah Weiss affair.

Hannah should have been a turning point. He'd
recruited her, for God's sake; had made what might
have been a career-ending fiasco a small but none-
theless decorative coup, giving the Park a channel
into the BND: a friendly Service, sure, but you
didn't have to be in John Bachelor's straits to
understand what friendship was worth when the
chips were down. And given all that had happened
since – Brexit, he meant – Christ: that young lady
was worth her weight in rubies. And it had all
been down to him, his idea, his tradecraft, so
when he'd learned he wouldn't be running her
– seriously, John? Agent-running? You don't think

that's a little out of your league? – he'd got shirty, he supposed; had become a little boisterous. Truth be told, he might have had a drink or two. Anyway, long story short, he'd been escorted from the premises, and when the Dogs escorted you from Regent's Park, trust this: you knew you'd been escorted. He might have lost his job altogether if they could have been bothered to find a replacement. As it was, the one morsel he'd picked up on the grapevine was that Snow White, which was what they were calling her now, had been farmed out to Lady Di's latest favourite: one Richard Pynne, if you could believe that. Dick the Prick. You had to wonder what some parents thought they were doing.

Bachelor yawned, his broken night catching up with him. Through the pub window he could see it trying to snow; the air had a pent-up solid grey weight to it, like a vault. If he had to spend the night in the car, currently Plan A by default, there was a strong likelihood he'd freeze to death, and while he'd heard there were worse ways to go, he didn't want to run a consumer test. Perhaps he should rethink approaching Solomon . . . Pity was tough to bear, but grief would be worse, even if he weren't around to witness it. But if so, he'd have to either come up with a story as to why he'd got nowhere tracing Peter Kahlmann or, in fact, try tracing Peter Kahlmann. It occurred to him that of the two options, the latter required less effort. He checked his watch. Still shy of noon, which gave him a little wiggle room. Okay, he thought. Let's try tracing Peter Kahlmann. If he'd got nowhere by three, he'd apply himself to more urgent matters.

And he did, as it happened, have an idea where to start.

A coffee shop just off Piccadilly Circus: a posh one where they gave you a chocolate with your coffee, but placed it too close to your cup, so it half-melted before reaching the table.

Hannah Weiss didn't mind. There was something decadent about melting chocolate; the way it coated your tongue. Just so long as you didn't get it on your fingers or clothes.

Richard Pynne said, 'So it'll go through like you asked. Make your transfer application. You don't have to mention the stalking thing. It'll be expedited, end of next week at the latest.'

'That's great, Richard. Thank you.'

She'd enjoyed working at BIS, but it was time for a change. If Richard hadn't come through, 'the stalking thing', as he'd put it, would probably have done the trick, but it was as well she hadn't had to go down that route. Julia, her line manager, would be horrified at the accusation; though of all the people who'd inevitably become involved, Julia would be easiest to convince of her own guilt. There was a certain kind of PC mindset which was never far away from eating itself. But more problematic would be being noticed for the wrong thing. Like all large organisations, the Civil Service hoisted flags about how its staff should report wrongdoing, but if you actually did so, your card was marked for life. It was hard not to feel aggrieved about that, even if the reported wrongdoing was fabricated.

Pynne said, 'I actually had a pastry earlier. Not sure I want a chocolate now.'

Because he was expecting her to, she said, 'Well, if you don't . . .'

He grinned and turned his saucer round so the chocolate was nearest her. Using finger and thumb, she popped it into her mouth whole. Richard watched the process, his grin flickering.

'You're okay with us meeting here?'

'Sure. I'll have to be back in the office in twenty minutes though.'

'That's okay. I just wanted to pass on the good news.'

They were of an age, or at least, he wasn't so much older that it looked unusual, the pair of them meeting for coffee. Nobody observing would have to make up a story to fit; they were just pals, that was all. He'd suggested, of course – back when they were building this legend – that he be an ex-boyfriend; still close, maybe on/off. And she'd given it genuine thought, but only for the half-second it took to reject it. The alacrity with which he'd agreed that it wasn't, after all, a great idea had amused her, but she'd taken care to keep that hidden. On paper he was her handler, and it was best all round if he thought that was the case in the real world too.

She supposed, if she were more important to the Park, they'd have given her someone with more experience; a father figure, someone like the man who'd recruited her in the first place. Pynne, though, was learning the game as much as she was; they were each other's starter partners, or that was the idea. A fun-and-games op; blowing smoke in a friendly agency's eyes, just to show you could, though European rules had changed in the years since Hannah's recruitment, and if nobody was expecting hostilities to break out, a certain amount of tetchiness was on the cards. So maybe her value to the Park was on an upward trajectory, but even so, she wouldn't be assigned a new handler now. It didn't really matter. The fact was, Hannah Weiss had been playing this game for a lot longer than Richard Pynne. And the handler the BND had matched her with had a lot more field savvy; but then, he knew Hannah was a triple, working for the BND, while the Park thought she was a double, working for the Park.

Maybe everyone would sit down and have a good laugh about all of this one day, but for the moment, it suited her real bosses that she be transferred to the office handling Brexit negotiations. It wasn't the world's biggest secret that Britain had been handling these discussions with the grace and aplomb of a rabbit hiding a magician in its hat, but, on the slim chance that somebody had a master plan up their sleeve, the BND wouldn't have minded a peek.

'So . . . Everything else all right?'

Hannah sipped her coffee, looked Richard Pynne directly in the eye, and said, 'Yes. Yes, all fine.'

He nodded, as if he'd just managed a successful debriefing. It was hard not to compare his treatment of her with that of Martin, who sometimes insisted on clandestine handovers in public places – the old ways are the best, Hannah; you have to learn how to do things the hard way; this is how we do a *drop*, Hannah; learn this now, it may someday save your life – and other times spirited her away for the evening; one of the brasher clubs round Covent Garden, where up-and-coming media types mingle with new-breed business whizz-kids. Those evenings, they'd drink champagne cocktails, like a September/May romance in the making, and his interrogation of her life was a lot less timid than Richard Pynne's. What about lovers, Hannah; fucking anybody useful? You don't have to say if you don't want to. I'll find out anyway. But she didn't mind telling him. When they were together, she didn't have to hide who she was. And not hiding who she was included letting him know how much she enjoyed hiding who she was; how much she enjoyed playing these games in public. Because that's what it was, so far; a fun-and-games op in one of the world's big cities. How could she not be enjoying herself?

'But don't ever forget, Hannah, that if they catch you, they'll put you in prison. That's when the fun stops, are you receiving me?'

Loud and clear, Martin. Loud and clear.

Now she said to Richard Pynne, 'I'll put my application in this afternoon. The sooner the better, yes?'

'Good girl.'

She finished her coffee, and smiled sweetly. 'Richard? Don't get carried away. I'm not your good girl.'

'Sorry. Sorry—'

'Richard? You have to learn when I'm teasing.'

'Sorry . . .'

And she left him there, to settle their bill; not looking back from the cold pavement to his blurred face behind the plate-glass window, like a woman who's just told her Labrador to stay, and won't test his mettle by flashing him kind-ness.

At Regent's Park the weather, to no one's surprise, was much the same as elsewhere in London; the skies sea-grey, the air chill, and packed with the promise of snow.

John Bachelor was having a conversation with a guardian of the gate, who in this particular instance was seated at a desk in the lobby. 'You're not expected,' she was telling him, something he was already aware of.

'I know,' he said. 'That's what "without appointment" means. But I'm not meeting with anyone,
I just need to do some research.'

'You should still book in ahead.'

He swallowed the responses which, in a better
life, he'd have had the freedom to deliver, and
managed a watery smile. 'I know, I know. Mea culpa.
But my plans for the day have gone skew-whiff, and
this is the one chance I have at redeeming the hour.'

His plans for the day had obviously involved
shaving and putting a clean shirt on, the woman's
non-spoken reply spelled out. Because those things
hadn't happened either. But she ran his name and
ID card through her scanner anyway, and evidently
didn't come up with any kill-or-capture-on-sight
instructions. 'It says you're in good standing,' she
said, with a touch too much scepticism for Bachelor's
liking. 'But I'd rather see your name on the roster.'

All or nothing.

'You want me to give Diana a ring?' He
produced his mobile phone. 'I could call Diana.
Sorry, I mean Ms Taverner. You want me to call
her? She can put you straight.'

For a horrible second he thought she was about to call his bluff, but the moment passed; gave him a cheery wave, he liked to think, on its way through the door. She did something on her keyboard, and a printer buzzed. Retrieving its product, peeling a label from the sheet, she clipped it onto a lanyard. 'That's a two-hour pass,' she told him. 'One second over, I send in the Dogs.'

'Thank you.'

'Have a nice visit.'

Seriously, he thought, passing through the detectors and heading for the staircase; seriously: Checkpoint Charlie must have been more fun, back in the old days. Not that he'd actually been there. On the other hand he knew what it was, and wouldn't mistake it for a Twitter handle.

He took the lift and headed for the library. He didn't have an appointment, it was true, because an appointment would have appeared on someone's calendar, and anything documented in the Park carried the potential for blowback of one sort or another. Bachelor's standing might be 'good', as the guardian of the gate had reluctantly verified, but 'good' simply meant he wasn't currently on a kill-list. If he actually did bump into Di Taverner, she might have him dropped down a lift shaft just for the practice. So no, no actual appointment, but he had rung ahead and made contact with one of the locals; asked if they could have a quick chat, off the books. In the library. If the local was around, that was.

He was.

They still called it the library, but there weren't books here any longer; only desks with cables for charging laptops. Bachelor settled in the corner furthest from the door, draped his coat on a chair, then went and fetched a cup of coffee from the dispenser, on his way back suffering a glimpse of a future that awaited him, one in which he haunted waiting rooms and libraries, anywhere he might sit in the warmth for ten minutes before being asked to move on. How had it come to this? What had happened to his life? He made a panicky noise out loud, a peculiar little *eck* sound, which he immediately repeated consciously, turning it into a cough halfway through. But there was only one other person in the room, a middle-aged woman focused on her screen, and she had earplugs in, and didn't glance his way.

At his table, he warmed his hands on the plastic cup. He didn't have his laptop – he'd left it in his car; a disciplinary offence, come to think of it – so opened his notebook and pretended to study his own words of wisdom. He must look like an illustration of how he felt: an analogue man in a digital world. No wonder it was leaving him behind so quickly. But others managed. Look at Solomon. Bachelor thought again of that cosy flat, its busy bookshelves, the active chessboard indicating Solomon's continuing engagement in struggle, even an artificial one, played out with himself. By any current reckoning, Solomon was of no account; part of the last century's flotsam, unless it was jetsam; discarded by a now unified state, washed up onto an island that had lately reasserted its insularity. But he still felt himself part of the game, enough to alert Bachelor that he'd thought he'd seen a drop. No, Bachelor corrected himself; Solly *knew* what he'd seen. He might have been wrong, but that was barely relevant. Solomon knew.

The name Peter Kahlmann stared up at Bachelor from the notebook in front of him.

So okay, it was true that he had designs on Solomon's sofa; on having somewhere to sleep that wasn't the back seat of his own car. But that didn't mean he couldn't pursue the trail in front of him to the best of his careworn abilities – he wasn't, when you got down to it, acting under false pretences. He was, in fact, acting under genuine pretences, and if in some eyes that might seem worse, it was the best he could manage in the circumstances.

'Bachelor?'

He started, alarmed that he'd been found out.

'It is you, right?'

And he admitted that indeed it was.

'Alec?' was how Bachelor had greeted him the first time they met. 'Do I detect a touch of Scots?'

'It's Lech,' Alec said. 'And no, I'm not one of the Scottish Wicinskis. But good catch.'

So yes, Alec Wicinski, born Lech, to parents themselves UK citizens, but both offspring of Poles who'd settled here during the war; named by his mother for the hero of the hour, Lech Wałęsa, which proved such a burden to the young Lech throughout a turbulent school career that he reinvented himself at university: Alec, good proper name, nothing off the wall about it. He'd since come to semi-regret the change, and now answered to both, depending on who was addressing him. That he had two names – two covers – both real – amused him. Made him feel more a spy than his Service card did.

Which stated, when run through a scanner, that Alec Wicinski was an analyst, Ops division, which meant he worked on the hub, except for those rare occasions when he sat in the back of a van, watching other people kick doors down. Afterwards, he'd be who you went to to find out why the door hadn't come off its hinges first kick, or where the stuff you'd expected to find behind it might be now.

Where John Bachelor had encountered him had been at the funeral of an ancient asset, who'd been a friend of Alec's grandfather, unless he'd been the grandfather of Alec's friend. Bachelor was hazy on the details, having launched himself wholeheartedly into the inevitable wake, but he'd made a point of scratching Wicinski's name on the wall of his memory cave. You never knew when a contact at the Park would come in handy.

Alec sat, and shook his head when Bachelor suggested coffee. 'You have a name that might interest me?'

'It came through one of my people,' Bachelor told him. Having people lent him weight, he thought. 'Might be something, might be nothing.'

'Are we currently in a movie?'

'. . . What?'

'It just sounds like movie dialogue, that's all. Might be something, might be nothing. I process information, John. It is John, right?' It is. 'So, all information's either useful or it's not. But none of it's nothing. What's the name?'

'Peter Kahlmann,' Bachelor said.

'And what's the context?'

Bachelor said, 'One of my people, I look after retired assets, I think I told you that, one of my people thought he saw him making a drop. Or taking a drop, rather.'

'A drop?'

'An exchange of some sort. A package. An envelope. Done surreptitiously in a public place.'

'Sounds kind of old school.'

'That's what I thought.'

'I didn't know they even did that any more. Whoever they are.' Alec scratched his head. 'And even if they did, that doesn't make it our business. Could be anything. Could be drugs.'

'A lot of drug money goes places where it becomes our business,' Bachelor said.

'Yeah, I know. Just thinking out loud. Who's the asset?'

'An old boy, one of our pensioners.'

'Behind the Curtain?'

'Back in the day, yes.'

Alec nodded. The eyes behind his glasses were dark, but lively. 'And where did he see what he says he saw? And where did the name come from?'

Bachelor ran through it all, start to finish. He didn't hide what he thought was possible: that Solomon Dortmund, who was sharp but ancient, might have witnessed an innocent stumble. But he didn't hide, either, that Solomon had seen such games played for real; that he'd played them himself, in places where, when you were caught, they didn't just make you sit out the next round.

'So why aren't you going through channels?' Alec said, when he'd finished.

'. . . Channels?'

'If this is real, and not just an old man's mistake, it should go on the record. You know how this works. There's a reason we keep intel on file. It's so we can see the bigger picture. This Kahlmann, somewhere down the line, if he turns out to be planning an acid attack on the PM's hairdresser, I don't want to be the one sticking my hand up and saying, oh yeah, we had a line on him, but it didn't go through channels so nobody noticed.'

Bachelor, freewheeling, said, 'If it's a mistake, it's a mark against Solly. And you're right, he's an old man. They decide he's being a nuisance, they might pack him off to one of those homes they have, where you're not allowed more possessions than'll fit in your locker, and everyone gathers in the home room for an afternoon sing-song. It'd kill him.'

'But if he's seeing things that don't really happen, maybe one of those places is where he ought to be.'

'Do you have parents, Alec?'

'Please. Don't play that card.'

'It's the only one I've got.'

Alec Wicinski scowled, then stared for a moment or two at Bachelor's coffee cup. Then said, 'Okay, here's what I'll do. I'll run the name through the records, see if it rings any bells. And if it does I'll let you know, and then you can take it through official channels, okay?'

'Thanks, Alec.'

'But don't tell anyone I made a pass at it first. We're not supposed do favours. Not even for people we don't actually know, but just bumped into at a funeral.'

'Hell of a funeral, though,' Bachelor said.

Alec grinned. 'It was,' he said. 'It was a hell of a funeral.'

Afterwards, Bachelor lingered in the library, drinking two more cups of coffee, then – inevitably – had to take himself off to find the nearest toilet. And as he did so, he had that sense of foreboding again; a glimpse of a life spent looking for facilities he could use. Brushing his teeth in car park lavatories. Lurking near department store bathrooms, trying to look like a customer.

For the first ever time, it struck him: if this was what he had to look forward to, should he maybe just bow out?

It wasn't a moment of illumination; more a taking on board of something found at the back of his mind. Not *the* answer, necessarily, because something might turn up, but still: a way out of his current predicament; a means of avoiding the humiliations piling up ahead, like a roadblock designed by Kafka. He could simply pull the switch. The thought didn't fill him with a sense of triumph, but the fact that it didn't fill him with dread struck the deeper chord. It was said that people who talked about killing themselves never actually did so. And he wondered if those people who did had had moments similar to this one; whether their first inkling that that big word, 'suicide', had specific relevance to themselves arrived not hand in hand with calamity but during an ordinary day; and whether it had felt to them, as it did to him, like opening an envelope addressed to The Occupier, and finding their own name on the letter within.

And then he shuddered and filed such thoughts away, though he knew that a seal had been broken, and that he'd be forced to dip into this dark jar again in the future, probably at night.

There was a bathroom down the corridor. After he'd peed, while he was washing his hands, someone else entered, and Bachelor spoke almost without intending to. 'Do they still have showers on this floor? I pulled an all-nighter. I could really do with cleaning up.'

'Next floor down,' he was told.

'Thanks.'

Next floor down was easily found. The build-ing's geography was coming back to him as he wandered: showers, yes, and wasn't this where the bunking-down rooms were, where staff could crash when they were under the hammer? In the shower room were cupboards with towels, and even overnight kits: toothpaste, toothbrush, soap. He stayed under water as hot as he could manage until his skin grew lobster-pink. Then brushed his teeth and dressed again.

He was working on automatic now. It barely constituted a plan. Back in the corridor he made his way towards the bedrooms. None were in use. He chose one, let himself in, and locked the door behind him. The room wasn't much bigger than the single bed it contained, but that was all he was interested in. He undressed again, climbed into the bed, and when he flipped the light switch, the room became totally dark; a chamber deaf to noise and blind to light. For the first time in weeks, Bachelor felt alone and completely secure. Within minutes he slept, and dreamed about nothing.

It didn't do to be a man of habit, so Martin Kreutzmer wasn't; varying the routes he took to work; shuffling the bars he frequented, and the shops he patronised with no discernible brand loyalty. Some days he wore a suit; others, he dressed like a student. But he contained multitudes, obviously – he was a handler, an agent-runner, and handlers are all things to all joes – so it wasn't surprising that some of his identities took a less stringent attitude: an identity hardly counted as such if it couldn't be broken down into lists. Likes/dislikes, favourite haunts, top ten movies. So when he was being Peter Kahlmann he did the things Peter Kahlmann liked to do, one of which was visit Fischer's every so often, because even agent-runners enjoy a taste of the homeland now and again. He'd barely sat, barely glanced at the menu, when the waiter was asking him, 'Did your uncle's friend get in touch?'

'. . . I'm sorry?'

'Mr Dortmund. One of our regulars, I'm surprised you've not crossed paths before. Though you're not usually here in the mornings, like he is.'

'Could you start at the beginning, please?'

Afterwards, he enjoyed his coffee break, to all outward appearance unbothered by the exchange: Yes, now he remembered; old Mr Dortmund – Solly, that was it – had indeed been in touch, and yes, it was lovely to hear from someone who'd known Uncle Hans in the Old Days. Not many of that generation left. And yes, thank you, a slice of that delicious torte: what harm could it do? He gazed benignly round, and cursed inwardly. What had he done to attract the attention of an old man? There was only one answer: the drop. If the old man had noticed this, he must have been in the game himself. And if he'd taken it upon himself to establish Martin's – Peter's – identity, maybe he still was. Maybe he still was.

Martin blamed himself. Here on friendly ground – more or less – his duties were mostly administrative, and the bulk of his time was spent schmoozing compatriot bankers and businessmen, who thought him something to do with the embassy. Hannah Weiss was his only active agent, and yes, he'd made a game of his dealings with her, partly so she could learn how things were done properly; partly because he got bored otherwise. Lately, though, the ground had been shifting. European boundaries were being resurrected; the collapse of the Union couldn't be ruled out. There were those who said it couldn't happen, and those who couldn't believe it hadn't happened yet, and as far as Martin was aware, similar groups of people had said similar things about the Wall, both when it went up and when it came down again. It wasn't like the Cold War was about to be re-declared. But still, Hannah's value as an agent could only increase in the future. It was time to stop playing games.

As for the here and now, the report she'd passed him, here in Fischer's, indicated that all was going to plan. Her move from BIS to the Brexit Secretary's office was in the bag. With that jump, her value to the BND would increase fivefold; no longer an amusing sideline, she'd be a genuine source of useful data. But even if that weren't so, he chided himself, he remained at fault for putting her in harm's way. Even amusing sidelines had to be taken seriously. Practising old-school spycraft on the streets of London was one thing; getting spotted doing it was another. Hannah's career to date might have been little more than a joke one Service was playing on another, but they wouldn't simply waggle a finger in her face if she was caught. And whoever this Solomon Dortmund was, he looked set to make that happen, if he hadn't done so already.

Seized by sudden urgency, Martin Kreutzmer paid and left. In the old days, he'd have had to head back to his office and set research wheels in motion; track this fox Dortmund to his den. But these days you could do all that on the move, which is exactly what Martin did, striding along the High Street, coat collar up against the wind; one glove dangling by a fingertip from his teeth as he squeezed information from his phone.

★

Back in the Park, Alec Wicinski was doing much the same thing.

Dark curly hair; glasses half the time; a need to shave twice a day, though needs didn't always must in his case; Alec was a tie-wearer, a reader and a walker; not one for hill and field or coastal path, but a pounder of city streets, his usual cure for the bouts of insomnia that plagued him being to march through London after hours. His fiancée, Sara, joked that she'd picked him up on a street corner in the middle of the night. They'd actually met through a mutual friend, the old-fashioned way. Alec once worked out that they were the only engaged couple he knew who hadn't met online, and still wasn't sure whether to be surprised by that, and if so, why.

Alec, as noted, was an analyst, and oppo research his specialist subject, 'oppo' being granted broad definition these days. The lines were wavier than they used to be, old rivalries nearer the surface, and anyone who wasn't spying for us was spying on us. That, at least, was the motto on the hub, where whistle-blowing was the worst of crimes. There was something about an enemy pretending to be a friend, or a friend pretending to be an enemy, that could be lived with; but that either kind could pretend to have a conscience was a play too far. The boys and girls on the hub knew things could get murky, and that dirty truths had to be buried deep to keep the soil fertile; dragging them to the surface did nobody good. Lech understood this, and any dirty truths he uncovered that he was unhappy about he shelved in an attic corner of his mind, alongside his memories of his grandfathers' generation; those who'd fled Poland before the occupation, and fought their war under foreign skies. Back then, there was no doubting who the enemy was. Things were black or they were white, and even when they weren't – when there was shading round the edges – you acted as if they were, because that was what life during wartime was like, especially when your country was overrun. You'd picked your side. You didn't get to dictate strategy.

Those foreign skies were his own now, but his

Polish extraction – at least, he'd always assumed that's what it was, though maybe it was some individual quirk all his own – kept history fresher in his mind than most of his colleagues managed. And whereas the general attitude among the boys and girls was that right would ultimately triumph, something in Lech's bones sang of doom, or whispered along with the chorus: he was in his job to prevent bad things happening, but couldn't entirely suppress the fear that sooner or later he'd fail, that they'd all fail, that their home skies would look down on cataclysm. His grandfathers had taught him this much: that if you expected things to get worse, history would generally see you all right. Not that he'd be thanked for broadcasting this round the office.

For the moment, though, he did what he could.

Peter Kahlmann. Alec had a few spelling variations up his sleeve, but that was the version he entered first, running a multiple-site search on a number of Service engines: foreign operatives, British civilians, persons of interest of any nationality. The breadth meant he couldn't expect a response any time soon, so he let his laptop get on with it, while he busied himself with a report on a recent op in the Midlands – seventeen arrests, and an armed assault on Birmingham International scotched at the planning stage. Preventing bad things happening: one for our side, he thought, and suppressed the inevitable comeback from his mental gremlin, *Nobody wins all the time.*

Outside, it was starting to snow.

The flat was off Edgware Road, in a pleasant block with railinged-off basement areas, almost all of which contained an army of terracotta pots with small, neatly sculpted evergreens standing sentry. Upper storeys boasted window boxes on most of the sills. At this time of year, they were little more than a gardener's memento mori; the odd scrappy fighter among them battling the winter, but most standing fallow, waiting the bad months out. As if in vindication of their decision, it was starting to snow as Martin Kreutzmer approached; big chunky flakes drifting lazily down, the way Christmas card artists prefer, and a nice change from the dirty sleet London usually conjured up.

Outwardly, the block maintained the appearance of a row of houses, each with its own front door up a flight of stone steps. Sets of doorbells were fixed to the brickwork, labelled by name, and Martin had no trouble finding the one he was after: No. 36, Flat 5. He looked up and down the road. There were few people, and the only moving traffic was out of sight: shunting up and down the Edgware Road. All he was doing, he told himself, was checking out the opposition. There remained the possibility that Solomon Dortmund was exactly who he said he was: a friend of Martin's uncle. Except Martin didn't have any uncles, and even if he did, they wouldn't have any friends. So maybe Solomon Dortmund was in play, which meant Martin had to find out who was pulling his strings. For his own part, he was fireproof: the worst the British Secret Service could do to him was purse its lips in his direction. But if Hannah was blown, he'd have to put her on the next flight out of the country.

First things first: Martin rang the bell. Old people respond to doorbells; ingrained politeness, combined with a sense of need: the need to show visitors they were up and dressed, mobile, compos mentis. It was possible he was projecting. Anyway, Solomon Dortmund didn't answer his bell, meaning the odds were he was out, which gave Martin a whole new set of options: act as if the worst had happened, and pull Hannah's ripcord, or carry on digging in case the whole thing turned out to be an old man's brain-fart. When in doubt, he thought, secure your joe; that was the bedrock of agent-running. Back home they'd throw their hands up and ask if he was getting scaredy-cat with age, but screw that: they weren't the ones who'd be carted off in a Black Maria if it all went wrong. He wasn't about to gamble Hannah's future just to keep the bean counters happy, so he was pulling the cord, and that was the decision he'd come to as the door opened and an old woman emerged, a dog in her arms, a shopping basket looped through one of them too. 'You are *such* a nuisance,' she was saying, and Martin could only presume she was addressing the dog. Confirmation arrived when she looked him directly in the eye. 'He is *such* a nuisance.'

'But a fine fellow all the same,' he told her. 'Let me get that for you.' Meaning the door, which he held while she made her slow way through: dog, shopping basket, a walking stick too, it turned out. 'Can I see you down the steps?'

'That would be kind.'

'Let me just fix this,' he said. 'Don't want to have to disturb anyone again.' He laid his gloves down to prevent the door shutting and then, to forestall any interrogation as to who he was visiting, and what the nature of his business was, kept up an unbroken commentary on dogs he had known while helping his companion to the pavement: was he a one for chasing squirrels? Martin himself had heard that terriers were the very devil for squirrels; had known one personally, hand on heart, that had learned to climb trees. Sweetest dog in the world, that quirk apart. Would rescue ducklings, and escort lost fledglings back to their nests, but squirrels: that dog had an issue with squirrels. By the time all was done, and she was heading off towards Marks & Spencer, Martin had almost convinced himself he'd known her years, such was the degree of fondness with which she took her leave. Dear boy. He headed back up the steps, retrieved his gloves, and closed the door behind him. Solomon Dortmund: Flat 5. Two flights up.

Must be a game old bird right enough, Martin thought, as proud of his command of English idiom as he was of his ability to get up the stairs without losing breath. He'd found no images of Solomon Dortmund on his quick trawl through the ether, but the one in his mind had the old man a robin: bright of eye and twice as perky, hopping up and down these stairs twice a day, for all he was eighty. Ninety? And here was his door, and Martin rapped on it, and again there was no response. This wasn't great tradecraft, but sometimes you rode your luck. Plan an operation, and it took you weeks. Grab an opportunity, and you could be back in your foxhole by teatime, mission accomplished. It was a good solid door, and a top-hole lock. There were spies out there, good and bad, who could find their way through a locked door, but Martin Kreutzmer wasn't one of them. He'd read a few books, though. He ran a hand along the top of the door frame and found nothing, then bent to the welcome mat. Who kept a welcome mat outside their front door? An old person. Or maybe just a hospitable person, he amended, and lifted the mat and found the spare key carefully taped to the underside. Solomon, Solomon, he thought. Thank you for that. He heard a noise downstairs and froze, but the noise – a door opening and closing – was followed by its own echo: someone going out onto the street. He looked at the key. Yes or no? He'd not have a better chance. Three minutes tops, he told himself. Just to find out who this geezer – this robin – thinks he is.

And he let himself into the flat.

And here was the snow they'd been expecting, thought Solomon; a few little flurries to start with, to make everyone sentimental about how pretty

London looked with its edges rounded, and then more intently, more seriously; this was snow with a job to do, snow that would cause everything to grind to a halt: buses and taxis, the Underground, the people, the shops, the law, the government. All these years gone by, and he still didn't know what it was with the British and snow. Pull on your boots, wear gloves, spread a little salt and put shovels in the hands of the right people: what was so difficult about that? But no, let any kind of weather turn up looking grim and the country went into shock. But ah well, he thought; ah well, at least he'd had the sense to notice which way the wind was blowing. So here he was, loaded shopping bags in each hand, and if the snow meant he was confined to his flat for a week, while the oafs on the council ran round like headless chickens, wondering what the white stuff was and how to make it go away again, at least he wouldn't be wondering where his next tin of sardines was coming from, or forced to reuse coffee grounds. That had happened before.

He had to put all his bags down to find his

door keys. They were never in the pocket you'd put them in; that was something else a long life had taught him, that keys were determined to drive you out of your mind, but ah, here they were, and he could perhaps fish them out without removing his gloves, but no, that wasn't going to happen: off come the gloves, Solomon. Off come the gloves, as if he were about to enter battle, when in fact his day's campaign was over: he had his shopping, he had his keys – yes, there they were, plain as daylight in his hand – and now all he had to do was carry this shopping up two flights of stairs and he could settle down in his chair while the outside world did its worst.

The door was open, the shopping bags lugged over the threshold, the door was closed again, the light was on. Solomon felt dizzy when this was completed, and was breathing hard. Nonsense to suggest that a little exertion was too much for him; but on the other hand, on the other hand. He had outlived everyone he had ever loved, and while he viewed a number of those still breathing with affection, he wouldn't miss them when he was gone as much as he'd delight in the company of those he'd be joining. And it was often the case, he reflected, that you had such thoughts at the bottom of a staircase. Once you'd reached the top, there were more immediate things to dwell on, such as the contents of his shopping bags. Tins of sardines and necessary pints of milk apart, a few treats had been included. An old man doesn't need chocolate. But an old man has every right to a few things he doesn't need, when the snow outside is falling hard, and no telling when he'd next make it to Fischer's. The dizziness passed, and he chuckled. What were a few more flights of stairs? His life so far, he'd long lost count of how many stairs he'd climbed. Everyone did, after the first few.

But here he was now, up both flights, and his front door awaiting him. Again, there was the problem with the keys, which turned up in the wrong pocket, second time of looking. A sorry business, this growing older every day. But moments later he was home; in his own warm flat where all his possessions waited, his comfortable chair, his

small library, his slippers, his life. He closed the
door, and would have taken his bags through to
the kitchen had something not struck him: not a
thought, not a sound, a smell; a stranger's smell
– there had been, possibly still was, someone in
his flat who should not be there; someone who
carried, as Solomon did, his own odour: sweat,
soap, all the undefinables we muster along the
way. Solomon's heart was hammering now; his
breathing rapid. Were they still here? The door
had been locked, was unbroken; a skilled burglar
could enter through a window, but not without
being seen from the street, surely, at this time of
day? He sniffed deliberately, but the smell had
been erased by odours from his shopping bags:
the fresh bread, the fruit, the minced lamb, the
cheese – the cheese? Was that what had snagged
his attention, the urgent clamouring of goats'
cheese? He reached out for the nearest shopping
bag and raised it head-high: sniffed again. *Ha!*
Goats' cheese! He had heard many tales of old
men frightened by their shadows, but this – this!
– he would not be living this down soon, even

if it remained his closely guarded secret, which it would. It would.

Solomon carried the bags to the kitchen then returned to the door, removed his coat and hung it on the stand. Hat too. He'd not be leaving again in a hurry; he could see through the window the snow drawing crazy patterns in the air. The streets would be thickly carpeted soon. He removed his shoes, and headed for the bedroom. Cheese was on his mind. That smell of cheese, already occupying the entire flat. In his bedroom he sat and, before putting his slippers on, cradled each foot for a while. Even through his socks he could feel the miles these extremities had carried him; travels carved into skin which didn't even feel like skin any more; felt like a thick plastic covering, onto which various lumps and ridges had been moulded. The body's journey, written on itself. He planted both feet on the floor and stood, and felt again that wash of dizziness he'd suffered at the foot of the stairs. Careful, Solomon. He reached out for support, and found the handle of the wardrobe door: that was better. Thumping heart, the smell of cheese. A shiver down his back. He should put something warm on, make some tea. There was a cardigan in the wardrobe, so he opened the door and a shape loomed out, sudden and dangerous. Something burst inside old Solomon, though the shape was only briefly there; it had gone, stepped past him, was through the door before Solomon had finished his journey. This had started many years before, very far away, and ended where the floor began. For a moment or two he lingered on the threshold of himself, but the possibility of rejoining his loved ones proved too beguiling to resist, so Solly stepped across whatever the boundary was, and closed the world behind him.

It was much later that Alec Wicinski checked his laptop for search results: he'd become caught up in several matters, each more urgent than a name-chase for an acquaintance. He wanted to get home: travel was going to be a bitch, with Tube lines down because of the snow (why? Why did snow affect the Underground?) and while he never minded walking, he didn't have shoes for the weather. He texted Sara, confirming their dinner date, filled out his time sheets, then called up the search engines he'd set in motion and scanned the hits: six Peter Kahlmanns, the length and breadth of Europe. Which didn't mean there weren't more, and – allowing for fake IDs – didn't mean there weren't fewer, but it did mean there were six that fell within the parameters of the chosen engines. And this wouldn't have been more than a passing observation were it not for something that rang a bad bell: loud and bastard clear.

One of the Peter Kahlmanns was flagged.

Flagging could have meant any number of things. It could have meant Peter Kahlmann was a friendly, an asset, a joe even; could have meant he was on a watch list; could have meant he had diplomatic status, and was to be immediately released if he turned up under a hooker's bed during a raid. But what it most definitely meant was, Alec would need a cast-iron reason for having looked him up in the first place. Running a search on a flagged target was like stepping on a tripwire: hard to tell whether you'd done any damage until you lifted your foot again. Everything might be okay, and the world go on as normal. Or you might find your leg blown to kingdom come. Life was full of surprises.

What was certain was that his favour for John Bachelor wasn't a secret any more. When you ran up a flag, someone in the Park saluted.

He cursed under his breath, then closed all the engines down, not even bothering to examine the particular Peter Kahlmann who'd taken the starring role in his extracurricular trawl. Some things it was better not to know. The bright side was that if Alec had stepped into anything especially messy, he'd not be finding out about it now; he'd have been hauled away and given the treatment the minute he'd fed the name into the system. So with any luck it was a procedural misstep, no more; one he'd answer for to Richard Pynne, his unlovable shift manager, come their end of the week catch-up, but not one that had capsized an op. He hoped to God not, anyway. Nothing to do now but cross fingers and hope.

As for Bachelor, he could go whistle. There were

favours you did for friends, and there were risks you took for family: Bachelor wasn't the latter and barely qualified as the former. The best Bachelor could hope for was that Alec didn't come looking for him. To point out the error of his ways.

He sighed, powered down and left. Outside, the snow was coming thick and hard: London didn't usually get like this, but when it did, it didn't mess about. It took him two hours to get home, and he missed his date with Sara by a mile. Worse things could happen. Still, that sense of history that Alec carried with him was flickering like a faulty lamp; reminding him that if you expected everything to go tits up, you'd rarely go far wrong.

He'd been woken late evening by a pounding on the door, and a sickening awareness that the Dogs had tracked him down. The pass the dragon at the gate had allowed him had expired hours ago. The place might be in lockdown by now, every corner turned inside out in the hunt for an irregular; a part-time milkman outstaying his welcome.

But you know what, John? That was the best sleep I've had in weeks. As he clambered out of bed, pulled his trousers on, opened the door, Bachelor felt, if not entirely refreshed, at least no worse than when he'd lain down, which was a significant improvement on recent events.

The Dog in question was called Welles, and was new to Bachelor. Time was, he'd kept up with the ground staff at the Park, for the sensible reason that you never knew when you might need a favour, but that was a big ask when you were part-time, and unwelcome on the premises.

'Man, you're in trouble.'

'Yeah, yeah. I've been there before.'

Except this time, it didn't seem such hostile territory. Welles, after delivering the requisite bollocking, gave him a pitying look and said, 'What happened, your wife kick you out?'

As it happened, yes. A while back, but as it could reasonably be seen as the starting pistol on his current circumstances, Bachelor did his best to look sheepish and nod.

'It's a skeleton crew tonight. London's at a

standstill because of the snow, and most were let go early. If anyone needs the bed, I'll be back to kick you out. But for now, get your head down. I'll clear it at the desk.'

'Thanks. I appreciate that.'

'Just don't do it again.'

So he climbed out of his trousers once more, and back into bed, and slept another eight hours, after which he really did feel like a new man; a man who wasn't afraid of what the day might hold. Riding his luck, he showered again, then went to the library and drank two cups of free coffee before leaving the building. The guardian of the gate, a new one, barely batted an eye as he turned in his pass. And then he was out in the world again, and it was a winter wonderland.

It always felt like that, first sight. Pour a couple of tons of snow onto the city streets, and that was all you could see: clean white brightness, all of London's sins forgiven, but it didn't take long for reality to seep through. There wasn't much traffic, but what there was had ploughed the snow, pushing oily puddles of slush into the gutters, and the pavements were punctuated with yellow patches and small piles of filth, where London's dogs had relieved themselves. By nightfall, once everything had iced over, romance would have given way to treachery, and every step you took, you'd be worried you'd end up flat on your back. But it was nice to have your philosophy borne out by the facts, thought John Bachelor, as he stood on a snowbound pavement and wondered what to do with his day.

His car was in a long-term near King's Cross, his suitcase in its boot, and this was as much of an address as he currently boasted. But an epic sleep and two showers had set him up well, even if his circumstances had witnessed no improvement overnight. He checked his phone for messages – to see if Alec, Lech, had got back to him – but he was all out of charge. Even that didn't depress him unduly. The snow had provided a time out; nothing would happen for the next little while, which gave him an alibi of sorts. He could make his way to Solomon's; tell him everything was in hand; that meanwhile, the snow made it impossible for him to get home to Potters Bar, and would it be possible to kip on his sofa? It was a soft way in. He wouldn't have to confess the car crash his life had become. Tomorrow, things would either look different again, or they wouldn't. Either way, he'd have had twenty-four hours to think things over, and at Solly's he was sure of a constant supply of coffee, maybe a good red wine towards the close of play.

So he walked. There were others on the streets, of course, some finding pleasure in the new white world; others plodding grimly through it as if looking forward to the next. On Edgware Road a car had crumpled into a lamppost, attracting an audience, and further along a snowball fight had broken out, apparently good-humoured, but it was early yet. When he reached Solomon's Bachelor rang the bell, but got no answer. He'd grown cold; his overcoat, too thin yesterday, definitely wasn't up to the mark today. He could hang around waiting for Solly to return, or see if he could get a neighbour to buzz him in. This dilemma didn't occupy him long, and third time of trying he was inside the building; soon after that, was on bended knee outside Solomon's door, retrieving the spare key. So far so good. He let himself in, called out but got no answer, so went to the kitchen to put the kettle on. Solomon wouldn't mind. Solomon had European manners. There was a stoppered bottle of red on the counter, and Solly wouldn't mind this either, Bachelor decided, pouring a quick glass. It wrapped itself around him like a shroud. He missed this: having a kitchen, having things in it, helping himself to them when he desired. The kettle boiled and switched itself off. Before seeing to it, Bachelor removed his coat and went to hang it up, which was when he noticed Solly's bedroom door hanging open. His heart sank. Doors, in Solomon's world, were kept closed. He took a step towards it, then changed his mind; returned to the kitchen, where he poured another, larger glass of wine. He drank it, soaking in the peace and quiet; the muffled quality of the snowed-on city. And then he went to discover the body of his friend.

★

No drops this time. No clever footwork. He needed to talk to Hannah, in person; no coded messages, no dead-letter shenanigans. All the fun and games of running an op on foreign soil: Martin had enjoyed teaching Hannah the old ways, but everything had become less funny once the old man dropped dead in front of him. He hadn't meant to scare the bastard; had meant to be long gone before he arrived home, but you couldn't plan for the cosmic fuck-up, and nobody expected to find himself hiding in a wardrobe. He'd left the flat as invisibly as he could, taping the spare key under the mat; had vanished into a whitening world which erased his footsteps behind him. And had kept both ears on the news ever since, and both eyes on the internet. But nothing yet about a body in a flat off Edgware Road. Which meant either that the body hadn't been found, or that it had been found and was being dangled from a tree in a clearing, while hunters waited in the undergrowth.

So he met Hannah at Liverpool Street Station the following morning, in the bookshop, browsing the thriller section. No surreptitious chat, just a surprised 'Gosh, fancy you being here,' then a wander into the crowd, thinner than usual because of the snow. The floor was slick with dirty foot-prints, and the tannoy's announcements were mostly of cancelled trains.

'It's best you don't know why I'm asking,' Martin said, 'but have any wires been tripped?'

'Something odd happened.'

'Tell me.'

She told him: Dick the Prick had mentioned his name, on the phone, the previous evening. 'Is there any reason why someone would be running a search on your handler?'

'You're my handler, Richard. Is this line secure, by the way?'

'It's fine. And yeah, sure, I'm your . . . handler, but I meant the other one, you know? The one you're only pretending to . . .'

'Pretending to report to.'

'Yeah.'

'No reason I can think of,' she'd told him. 'Why?'

She'd asked the question, though the answer was obvious: because someone had done precisely that. Run a search.

Peter Kahlmann was harmless, as far as the Park was concerned; a mediocrity the BND were using to run Hannah, their unimportant mole in an unexciting branch of the British Civil Service. And Peter Kahlmann would carry a little weight if leaned on; Peter Kahlmann wouldn't break at the first hint of pressure. But Peter Kahlmann wasn't indestructible, and if the Park chose to test his strength, he'd splinter and crack eventually, and there – peeping out from the broken shell – would be Martin Kreutzmer, and Martin Kreutzmer was a much more interesting character than Peter Kahlmann. For a start, Martin Kreutzmer wouldn't be running an unimportant mole like Hannah Weiss, which meant that the Park's double agent might require a little more attention herself.

Richard Pynne had said, 'So he hasn't said or done anything funny lately? He doesn't suspect that you're not what you claim to be?'

Every triple has moments like this: when they

have to consider, for a moment, who and what they claim to be. It largely depends on who they're talking to at the time.

But Hannah had just said, 'Nothing's changed. It's not like he's a big deal or anything. I think he regards running me as a chore he's been lumbered with.'

And now, in Liverpool Street, Martin said to her: 'Good. That's good.'

It wasn't good, but you never tell a joe the ground just got swampy.

He asked her to talk while he thought, and she launched into a work anecdote while they paced the station, stepping round or breaking through the queues forming at coffee stands. She was good at this, he registered, even as his mind chewed over other fodder. Whether she'd had this story up her sleeve, whether it had actually happened, whether she was improvising: didn't matter, she delivered it like a natural. And it washed through her while they marched, providing cover for his pondering.

Martin hadn't wanted the old man to die, but

these things happened. And if Solomon Dortmund hadn't died then, he'd have died at the first opportunity; the next time a shock was delivered to his door – a backfiring motorbike, a peal of thunder, a telephone, a doorbell. So what mattered now was whether anything could put Martin on the scene. Because he'd thought himself bulletproof, here in bumbling old Blighty, but if the Park got wind that a BND operative had been present when a Service asset died, there'd be retribution. How harsh this might be he wouldn't want to guess, but nor would he want to be there when guessing became unnecessary.

And Hannah needed to be secured too. His own position might be in jeopardy, but Hannah's safety was paramount – the joe always came first.

He said, 'How far would Pynne stick his neck out for you?'

'Richard? Pretty far, I think.'

'And if that wasn't far enough?'

Hannah thought about it, surveying the morose crowds of winter travellers. 'I could get him to stick it out further.'

'Let's hope it doesn't come to that. But do what you have to.'

'What do you need?'

'Find out who ran the search on Peter Kahlmann.'

She hugged him, made a loud goodbye; turned to wave when she was ten yards off, and he stood there watching her go: an uncle, a family friend, an innocent colleague, with a rolled-up newspaper under his arm.

The ground was swampy, but once he had the name of whoever had been checking his cover story out, he'd know what to do. If it had rung Pynne's bells, it must have come from within Regent's Park, but Pynne himself obviously didn't know why it had happened. Which might mean it had come from up the ladder, above Pynne's head, which probably meant game over: that Martin and Hannah would have to up sticks. But if it was someone lower down – someone who'd wandered off reservation on their lonesome – well. There might be other ways of solving the problem. Martin was old school, and rarely indulged in dirty work, but there were others within reach, a phone call away, who had different skills, different talents. They could turn a man's life upside down without laying a finger on him. If that happened to you, you'd quickly forget whatever extra-curricular games you'd been playing. You'd be too busy trying to plug the leaks you'd sprung, and hoping the damage wasn't permanent.

He left Liverpool Street, noting that the sky overhead was still a grey vault, and the air still bit back when you breathed it. There'd be more of this weather before there was less. He wasn't entirely sure the English language would bear that construction, but it sounded right in his head, and there was no one around to correct him.

John Bachelor sat for a while, drinking the wine, deciding he might as well eat. Solomon had been shopping; there were bags of food in the kitchen, still unpacked. Fresh bread, cheese; chocolatey treats. Tins of sardines. There was no point letting it go to waste. And nothing he could do right now about reporting Solly's death: his phone was still uncharged, and his charger was in his car. There was a department to ring in these circumstances, and a telephone in the flat, but Bachelor didn't know the number by heart, couldn't read it on his powerless phone, and tracking it down would mean talking to half-a-dozen suspicious civil servants. No, he'd sit a while before putting it all in motion: the necessary investigation, the endless reports, the winding down of Solomon's afterlife – his Service pension, his flat.

He went to take another look at the body. There were no signs of violence, and it was clear from the shopping that Solly had not been in the flat long when he died. Bachelor, not a doctor, reached the obvious conclusion: Solly had over-exerted himself doing an emergency shop, and this was the result. It was sad but it must have been quick, and among other things meant that Bachelor no longer felt obliged to indulge Solomon's final whimsy. The drop, the *pas de deux* Solomon thought he'd seen in Fischer's, had been nothing more than an ancient asset's final glimpse down the twists of Spook Street. Even if Bachelor put it on file, there'd be no follow-up; it would be dismissed as an old man's fantasy. Alec, if he'd run Kahlmann's name through the databases yet, had done so as a favour to Bachelor; he wasn't putting it through channels. So the drop could be quietly dropped, which meant that Solomon's passing would cause no more a ruffle than a passing pigeon. All Bachelor needed to do was write up today's one-sided visit, sign his name, and attend the funeral.

A stray thought wafted past, and whispered in his ear.

He dismissed it and made a cheese sandwich; ate looking down from Solomon's window to the muffled street below. It was warm inside; heating was paid by direct debit, from a Service account, and as this had been set up in the days before austerity – when people were valued for what they had done, rather than dismissed out of hand for being no longer capable of doing it – it was a generous monthly sum, ensuring Solomon need never grow cold. Like everything else to do with Bachelor's charges, the process was automatic and unquestioned. That was one thing about the Civil

Service: once it decided to do something, it carried on doing it. It would march on, indestructible, and sooner or later would probably inherit the earth, though when it did, it wouldn't do anything with it that it hadn't already been doing for centuries.

His sandwich eaten, Bachelor remained where he was, mulling options. As usual, there weren't many available. But for now, at least – warm and comfortable – he was in no hurry to exercise choice; he'd just sit for a bit and watch the snow. In the other room lay Solomon Dortmund, but that was okay. The old man had learned patience in life, and there was no reason why this virtue should abandon him now.

The snow lingered for days, hardening to ice on the pavements, the better to keep a grip, and though traffic reasserted itself eventually, it did so with a chastened air, reminded of its place in the great chain of being: the car was king of the road, but only while the weather allowed. Shops that had been closed opened up, and opportunist roadside vending vans moved on. In Regent's Park, the hub had maintained its quiet buzz throughout the hiatus, but the surrounding offices were only just coming back to life, proving what Alec Wicinski and his colleagues had long known: that actual work continues untroubled, regardless of management's presence. As for Alec himself, he hadn't turned up that morning, causing troubled glances among the boys and girls of the hub. Unexplained absence was a cause of concern in their world.

In her office, Lady Di was grilling Richard Pynne.

'When did it come to light?'

'During yesterday evening's sweep.'

'And there'd been no previous hint of . . . anything?'

Pynne shook his head.

He hadn't been at the Park lately, frozen lines having made his commute near impossible, but he'd bravely struggled into town to meet Snow White the evening before last. He'd worried when he got her call, an emergency-only code, and had spent the expensive cab ride picturing any manner of calamity. In his imagination, she was being hauled into a cellar by disgruntled BND operatives. So to find her fine – perky, even – was more than a relief; it was cause for celebration.

'I'm sorry, Richard. I got a case of the frights. But I'm okay now.'

'It happens.' Their hug went on longer than he'd expected. 'Joes in the field, you're allowed to get the frights. That's what I'm here for. To make them go away again.'

Instead of coffee and a chocolate, they'd snuggled down in a bar off Wardour Street, and at her suggestion he'd ordered tequila slammers. Just the thing to chase the jitters away. And a legitimate expense, almost certainly.

Inevitably, things had become hazy towards the end. She'd asked, he remembered, about what he'd said the previous day; those mysterious questions concerning Peter Kahlmann, and he'd explained, fuzzily, that he couldn't go into details; that a flag had been raised because someone on the hub had run a search on Kahlmann, and no, he couldn't tell her who. *Clashified* information. She'd laughed: You sound like James Bond. *On Her Majesty's Shecret Shervish*. He'd laughed too: I preferred Roger Moore. It had been a crazy evening. Crazy. But he was almost certain he'd not mentioned Alec Wicinski by name. Which would have meant nothing to Hannah anyway.

So yesterday he'd stayed off work using snow as an excuse, but the truth was he'd got home so loaded, he'd barely been able to crawl out of bed in the morning. His first few hours had been spent cradled over the toilet. Touch of flu, he'd phoned in: Yeah yeah yeah. And then, come evening, when he was just about upright again, the results of the weekly remote sweep of the boys' and girls' laptops came in.

Which was when the problem with Wicinski came to light.

Pynne said, 'The laptop's been in his sole possession. The download took place outside office hours, but that's neither here nor . . . Thing is, he's claiming not to know anything about it, but he would, wouldn't he? And if anyone else gained access to his machine, that in itself's a disciplinary offence. These things are beyond classified. That's the first thing they tell you when you're given one.'

This hadn't prevented laptops being left in cabs or on trains, but that wasn't the issue right now.

Di Taverner said, 'And it's illegal?'

'Child porn,' said Pynne. 'It's . . . they're saying it's pretty disgusting.'

'Yes, the clue's in the name.' She glanced towards the hub, and half-a-dozen faces turned quickly away. Sighing, she reached for the switch that frosted her glass wall. 'Could it have been planted remotely?'

'IT says yes, technically, but it would require serious, state-of-the-art intervention. Another Service might have the wherewithal to hack into one of our laptops and dump that stuff there from a distance, but it's not something a kid's done in his bedroom. And that being so, why would they? Why would another Service want to frame Wicinski?'

'What's he working on?'

'Nothing to put anyone's back up.'

'You're sure?'

Pynne was sure, or at least, he was sure that was the answer he wanted to give. Coincidences happened, everyone knew that. Had he mentioned Alec's name to Snow White? He was pretty certain not. Besides, Alec was on his team, his name cropped up all the time. Alec this and Alec that. That was the nature of being a manager: your team was always on your radar.

'Where is he now?'

'Dogs.'

Through the frosted wall came the dim suggestion of movement. That would also be the Dogs, here to ransack Lech Wicinski's workstation and dismantle his hardware. His locker would have been turned out by now too. Either more evidence of his moral corruption would be found, or he'd be shown to have buried it completely – this slip-up aside, that is.

'I can believe he gets off on that stuff,' she said. 'Everyone has a dark side. What I don't understand is why he'd download it onto our laptop.'

Pynne didn't know either. But he said, 'If you

get away with something for long enough, you start to think you're too clever to be caught.'

'So he's been doing it for a while?'

There were any number of pitfalls here, chief among them, that he'd be called to account for not having rumbled Wicinski's predilections earlier. 'There've been no indications of aberrant behaviour. He's always passed the psych tests. But . . .'

'But if it wasn't possible to disguise the urge, we'd all know who the paedophiles were,' she finished. 'Jesus, Richard.'

It crossed his mind to offer comfort, but he wisely kept his mouth shut.

She said, 'He'll have to go on suspension. While the Dogs do whatever they need to do.'

Pynne said, 'It's a criminal offence. Shouldn't we pass it to the Met?'

'And enjoy another season of spook-bashing? I don't think so. Things are bad enough without gifting the tabloids their headlines. No, we'll handle this in-house. If he's got any sense, he'll come clean without letting the whole thing drag on too long.' She defrosted the window. 'And then it'll be just like we like it. Everything out in the open.'

He could rarely tell, with Lady Di, where the irony stopped.

She shifted gear. 'How's Snow White coming along?'

'Fine,' he said. 'Her transfer's come through. She starts in the Brexit office Monday.'

'And it's all going smoothly? The two of you?'

'Yes.'

'Good. It's not an easy business, running an agent. Even on friendly soil. If this continues to go well, we'll think about expanding your brief. But I'll need to be sure you're up to it.'

'Thank you.' He stood to go, but paused at the door. 'What'll happen to him? Alec?'

'If he turns out guilty?'

He nodded.

She said, 'Well, we can't sack him. Not without inviting attendant publicity. But he can't stay here, obviously. Not that he'd want to, now his secret's out in the open.' She reached for her laptop, tapped in her password. 'Just as well we've somewhere we can put him.'

'Oh,' said Pynne.

'Yes,' said Diana Taverner. 'Man's got a nasty kink. Slough House should be right up his street.'

And the snow stays where it is, and the weather doesn't turn, and the streets remain cold, and the days are dark from dawn to dusk. In different parts of London, different people feel different things. Alec Wicinski is mostly numb, dumbfounded by the speed with which his life has spiralled into hell; while Martin Kreutzmer has the sense of having narrowly avoided disaster, and can now see a clear path ahead, leading steadily upwards. Hannah has started in her new role, where it is apparent she will have access to information useful to the folk back home; together, the pair look set to enjoy many a triumph. And it's a pleasure to hoodwink another Service, especially when that Service thinks it's hoodwinking you. Contemplating the last few days, Martin gives silent thanks to the BND's sneaker team, who can walk through the Park's firewalls and leave packages in laptops the way couriers leave parcels in dustbins – without notice, and undetected – but if he spares a thought for the poor bastard on the receiving end, it's a brief one. Martin has been playing this game a long time, and knows that, like those of politicians, all spies' lives end in failure. The best among them fade away with no one having suspected their true calling; for others, the end comes sooner, and that is all. It is part of the game. He lights a rare cigar and wonders what his next move will be. There's no hurry. The game lasts forever.

As for John Bachelor, he spends a lot of time at Solomon's window, looking down on what once were Solomon's streets. Solomon himself has been taken away, of course. An ambulance removed the body; a police officer came and took notes. Bachelor faked nothing, just described what had happened: he'd arrived to check on the old man, and the old man didn't come to the door. There was a spare key taped under the mat . . . His cover held up. There is an actual company, existing on paper, by which he is employed to visit the elderly and infirm, ensuring their needs are catered for, their lives secure and intact; the sort of service once provided free by society, before the 1980s happened. There'll be a funeral next week. He's called the numbers in Solomon's address book, kept by the phone. He's booked a room in a pub, and will put money behind the bar.

But he hasn't informed the Park. That stray thought that wafted past him, the same hour he found Solomon's body, returned, and returned again, and somehow clarified into intention. He has not informed Regent's Park that Solomon Dortmund is dead. So Solomon's pension will continue to be paid, and Solomon's flat will continue to be warm. It will only be for a short while, he tells himself; just until he has found his feet again, and it's not precisely corruption – is it? – more administrative streamlining. He's a free-floating irregular, poorly paid and unsupervised; if he chooses to keep his reports free of burdensome detail, that is up to him. It's not like anyone else is keeping an eye on his milk round. And he will do his job better, be more alert to his charges' needs, if he isn't worrying about his own circumstances; if he has somewhere to lay his head at night.

It occurs to him that he never heard back from Alec Wicinski, but that's a detail that has ceased to matter, and it won't bother him long.

And meanwhile the streetlights come on, and the view from the window thickens and slows. He remains where he is for a while, fascinated by the world he is no longer locked out in. There are no guarantees, he knows; his stratagem could be discovered at any time, and then he'll be for the high jump. Right now, though, John Bachelor is warm, he is fed; there is wine in Solomon's larder. In a minute, he'll go pour himself a glass. But for now he'll sit and watch the quiet snow.